THE KNOCKER

Jack Rigby

*To
Geraldine
Happy Birthday
25/05/2016
Jack Rigby*

2QT (Publishing) Ltd

First Edition published 2015 by

2QT Limited (Publishing)
Unit 5 Commercial Courtyard
Duke Street
Settle
North Yorkshire
BD24 9RH

Cover photograph: Jack Rigby

Printed by Charlesworth Press

A CIP catalogue record for this book is
available from the British Library

ISBN 978-1-910077-59-7

DEDICATION

To my Dad. Thanks for everything.

Contents

The Story: Part Two

The Story: Part Three

Chapter 1
THE PHONE CALL

IT WAS A hot day. A solitary white cloud sailed in the clear blue sky as the sun beat down.

The house had its windows open but it was still uncomfortably warm inside. He came into the kitchen; it was clean, neat and tidy with everything in its place, but dated and tired. He opened the back door to allow a draught through the house and caught sight of the birds, two fledglings, in the garden. The mother bird, a robin, perched on a lower branch in the cool shade of an elm tree looked over her fledglings as they hopped about the lawn. He stepped out onto the small patio and watched them for a moment before returning inside.

The young robins continued to play, hopping over the grass. Suddenly the mother bird looked down as one of her fledglings took to the air and flew through the wide-open doorway.

The young bird couldn't get out. It started to panic, tweeting, flapping, fluttering about, beating its wings up against the window, calling for its mother. He heard it and came back through into the kitchen. He managed to catch the bird and, holding it gently in his cupped hands, whispered to it softly. He kept the little thing calm as he carried it outside then opened his fingers and let the robin hop up onto the windowsill. The mother bird flew closer, landing on a pink-flowering rhododendron, calling to her fledgling.

Together, the birds flew away.

Ever after, when the little robin saw him through the windows it would fly down to the house, settle on a windowsill and peck at the glass, tapping until it got his attention. As always, when he heard it he would stop whatever he was doing, go outside and give it a treat.

⚭ ⚭ ⚭

The phone rings late at night; you fear the worst.

I was abroad, in bed asleep when the phone rang. Drowsy, in a haze, I reached over and fumbled as I put it to my ear and heard a female voice tell me, 'He has two days to live.'

The man with a robin for a friend was dying.

Early morning, I picked up the phone and rang round the operators. I got lucky and managed to get a flight leaving later that day.

I boarded the Airbus A380 that would take me halfway round the world and sat down in an aisle seat next to a blonde woman with pendulous breasts and rolls of fat straining the material of her white cotton blouse. I buckled my seat belt and caught the overpowering scent of her perfume and the faint smell of stale sweat that her perfume didn't quite overpower. A stick-thin man wearing a bright-green polo shirt and tan trousers sat in the window seat staring out over the runway and the last of the luggage going into the plane's underbelly, but it was obvious from his demeanour that his mind was elsewhere; as was mine.

No sooner had the plane taken off than the flight attendants came round serving food. I wasn't hungry, declined the tray laden with polystyrene containers and plastic cutlery and asked for a Martini. As I sipped my drink, I tried not to watch the fat woman scoff everything edible on her tray ... except the fruit salad. But as I avoided looking at her, I couldn't help noticing the thin man with the green polo shirt. He was pushing a pea slowly backwards and forwards round his tray with a white plastic fork. I knew how he felt. The fat woman noticed too, nudged him overly hard in the ribs and told him to stop.

Two stewardesses came down the aisle with a trolley and removed the dinner trays. I finished my drink, handed them the empty cup, settled back and tried to sleep but couldn't. I messed with the entertainment system; I watched various movie clips; I fiddled with my iPad, fought an ongoing battle with my right elbow against the obese woman's flabby left for possession of the armrest and simply wished the time away.

At last the plane landed.

It took an age to get through passport control, even longer in the crowded baggage hall to get my case. Other passengers were scrambling about picking up their luggage but where was mine? The fat woman stood in front of me touching up her lipstick, her husband beside her in his bright-green polo shirt struggling with a pair of pink suitcases. My bag appeared, I dodged past them, lifted it off the carousel and hurried on through the Nothing to Declare lane, hoping there wouldn't be a queue at the car-hire desk. There wasn't.

I parked the rental car, a little red Hyundai, and dashed through the pouring rain across the car park into the hospital. I found the ward and saw him straight away through the window at the back of the nurses' station. He lay, eyes closed, mouth open, his face the colour of lead. A wooden wedge held one of the double doors open to the single room.

I went over to the side of the bed and could only whisper, 'I'm here,' as I looked upon him. His eyes didn't so much as flicker at the sound of my voice. Sorrow gripped me but as I pulled a plastic chair over and sat down there was also joy. At least I'd made it in time; he was still alive and I was here for him.

I stayed with him for a long time, leaning over the bed, gently holding his hand, carefully avoiding the needles and tubes sticking out of his veins, but he never opened his eyes or spoke. Eventually I whispered a tearful goodbye and left.

As I drove from the hospital to his house, I passed a fish and chip shop. I pulled the Hyundai over, stopped the engine and went inside. I hadn't realised how hungry I was. I unravelled the paper and ate half the fish supper as I sat in the car. I finished off the rest in the kitchen back at the house while waiting for the kettle to boil to make a cup of tea. It was strange seeing only one cup on the clean work surface by the sugar bowl; it looked rather lonely. Where was his cup? He wasn't known to refuse a cuppa if someone was making one. He liked his tea white and weak; I preferred mine dark and strong.

Next morning I woke early, took a shower, dressed and headed back out to the hospital. The sky was grey, the day dull, a fine drizzle coming down. The wipers beat intermittently on the windscreen as I drove. The little red car smelled of fish and chips. Happy days, I thought.

The window behind the nurses' station had the blinds closed. I walked into the room; he was sitting up in bed and two nurses were giving him a wash. His eyes were open. As he saw me, the merest flicker of a smile appeared on his face.

'Hello, son,' he managed to croak. His dry lips moved to add, 'What are you doing here?' but didn't; too exhausted, too frail to say any more, his head flopped back onto the stack of white pillows. I stood at the bottom of the bed doing what I imagine most people do when they find themselves in this situation: pretending everything is going to be all right. I put on a cheerful act and kept my conversation light while the nurses finished up.

He fell asleep when the nurses left and I sat down on the hard plastic chair, holding his hand in mine. He woke a few times, and I gave him a drink and held it while he sipped from a straw. He seemed to like those small cartons of vanilla-flavour yoghurt drink best.

When I went home that night, I stopped at the twenty-four-hour chemist. I hadn't realised just how expensive those yoghurt drinks were but the pharmacist told me they were a complete meal in themselves and very nutritious, so I bought a bagful, mostly vanilla flavour, and paid with my card.

I arrived at the hospital the next day, thinking I might not find him alive but no, it was the same routine: a nurse washing his face, me coming through into the sterile white room, saying jovially while I felt anything but, 'How you doing today, Dad? You're looking a lot better,' and him barely able to reply, 'Hello, son.' The nurse finished, took the red washing bowl away and left me to sit and talk while my dad fell back to sleep. How much he heard I'll never know but every now and then a peacefulness settled over him, replacing the grim rigour, and I hoped my words had taken him to a nicer place.

Day after day passed like this but my dad was still alive.

On day number eight – you can't help but number and keep track of the days at times like these – I was late getting to the hospital. When I set off the fuel light was flashing on the Hyundai's dashboard. I needed to stop for petrol. I was grateful for the warning sticker on the car's petrol flap saying 'Unleaded' as I nearly filled the tank with diesel. Again, I paid with my card, thinking I must find time to get to a bank and get some cash.

My dad was alone in the sterile room, awake, sitting up in bed when I walked in. He looked at me with a shadow of his old cheeky grin and I saw the faintest twinkle in his eye. I felt a tug on my heart as he said, 'Hello, son,' and slowly managed to finish the sentence, 'How are you doing?'

Today it was his turn to do the talking. He told me he didn't want to be in hospital. He didn't want to stay in this stuffy, impersonal room, all alone with strangers poking and prodding him when he didn't want to be poked and prodded, even if they were only doing their job. He told me, 'I want to go home, to the comfort of my house.'

I arranged his discharge with the doctors.

A clever bed with electric controls and buttons that you could press to make things go up and down arrived at my father's house, along with a fancy vibrating mattress, oxygen bottles and an assortment of other medical paraphernalia. I moved the downstairs furniture round so the bed could fit next to the window. My dad would be able to look over the garden at his plants, watch the thrushes splash in the concrete bird bath on the lawn and the blue tits peck at the fat balls and steal the seeds from the bird feeder hanging on the rhododendron bush.

The ambulance drew up outside the house. The paramedics carried my father through to the bed. As they were getting him settled, both commented on what a nice view he had over the garden. 'You'll be all right here,' they said as they sorted his pillows. I hoped so.

I saw the paramedics out and, standing at the front door, thanked them before they left. When I returned my father was sitting up in bed, his head resting on the pillows, face slightly turned towards the window, a contented smile upon his face. He was glad to be home. A robin redbreast sat on the windowsill, head cocked to one side, looking in.

Chapter 2
THE STORYTELLER

IT WAS FAINT but I could see a very slight improvement in my father every day. He was getting ever so slightly stronger … I wasn't. I thought I could look after and take care of him, I really wanted to. After nearly three weeks I woke up and realised I was kidding myself. Caring for him during the day, up all hours of the night, was having its toll. I was going round like a zombie, a danger to my father and a danger to myself.

Over the next few days, I discussed the matter with my dad. As poorly as he was, he understood the situation and when I mentioned a care home he pretended it was a good idea. Kind and considerate to the end, he could see I was all in and couldn't go on coping like this.

I had done my best to look after him and that was good enough for him.

I found a nursing home, once a stately manor but now modified inside and adapted for its new purpose. Outside were extensive gardens with plenty of mature trees, well-stocked flower beds and a rather large, long lawn running down to woodland. A female member of staff told me that wild deer often roamed in the grounds.

The same woman took me inside to see what would be my father's room; it was a good size, decorated in neutral colours, with lots of windows so he could look out. There was an electric buzzer by the bed that he could press any time and the staff were on call twenty-four-seven. I got his special mattress, oxygen bottles and medical supplies sent over and moved him in. Overall, it was a fine place. I still had to take myself into the toilet though, where I cried at the thought of him being in a care home.

On the first day I stayed with him until late at night and was torn in two. I didn't want to leave him but I was out on my feet. I needed sleep. Near midnight I said, 'Dad, I'll have to go now.'

He looked up sadly from his pillows and replied softly, 'What will I do when you've gone, son?'

I said, 'Dad, it's nearly midnight. You need to get some beauty sleep otherwise you'll start to look old and the nurses won't fancy you any more.' This didn't raise a smile.

He looked at me feebly. 'But what if I can't get to sleep?'

I took a second before I replied and still to this day don't really know why I said, 'This is what we'll do, we'll write a book together. To do that, we'll need something interesting to write about. You can lie there in bed' – that was basically all he could do – 'and think of something we can write about.'

'What if I can't think of anything?'

'Surely, in all the eighty-nine years you've been on this planet you must have come across something a little interesting? Just think again and see what you can come up with.'

I gave him time. 'Well, have you thought of anything yet?'

'No,' he answered.

'I don't think you're trying hard enough. Think again,' I said with a gentle smile and again gave him a minute or two before asking, 'Well, have you come up with anything?'

'Yes,' he said. I was about to ask what when his eyelids closed and he fell into a comfortable sleep. I tucked the quilt round him, left and drove home; on the way I thought about how I didn't want to leave him but how much I was going to enjoy an unbroken night's rest.

$$\text{\Huge XXXX}$$

Next morning I woke refreshed; the fog had cleared from my brain. I got out of bed, showered and grabbed a piece of toast before jumping into the Hyundai. As I drove, the sun was shining, the sky was blue, the trees were in full leaf and, as I turned into the drive of the nursing home, a deer came bounding out of the woods and across the lawn.

I went into Dad's room. The staff had washed and dressed him and got him into an armchair. Although he sat stooped and frail, it was a treat to see him out of bed and there was a look about him, a definite sense of purpose.

'Good morning. Come and sit down close to me. About last night,' he said softly, 'I have a story to tell you.' He looked kind of pleased with himself … or as pleased as a dying man can look, I guess.

'That's good. What's the story about?' I asked, pulling up a chair by his side.

'It's about a rather peculiar man. I remember his first wife; she was a very pretty lady.' He looked up slowly, as if bringing her to mind. 'She had lovely auburn hair but went a bit funny and killed herself.'

'That was a shame,' I said.

'Yes, it was,' he replied. 'But she is only the beginning of the story.'

And so he began to tell his tale.

With the telling, the tale unfolded and a question came to mind. I started to ask, 'How did you…' but he slowly, weakly, raised his hand to silence me. 'You will only spoil the story if you interrupt.

Can your question wait until the end?'

My question could, so for the next few days I sat by his side, held the cartons of yoghurt drink when his mouth got dry, watched him sip from the straw, didn't interrupt and listened to his feeble, gentle voice as he slowly told his tale.

He was dying. I was lucky – I was there and heard him tell a story.

THE STORY: PART ONE

Chapter 3
RICH LORD, POOR MAN

ANOTHER ANNIVERSARY. SHE was having a bad day and sought comfort in the oblivion of sleep.

Open eyes unblinking, crisp linen sheets grasped beneath her chin, she lay rigid, staring blindly up into the blackness of the room seeing images of her twins. In the darkness her stillborn babies came to life, shape-changing from crying infants to laughing boys, into fine young men dressed in Savile Row suits. She found solace in this false imagery but her heart still ached.

Unable to bring her children into the world alive, she blamed herself, believing she had failed as a woman, failed as a mother. Her eyes remained wide, staring, feeding off the images while her body hungered for the respite of sleep.

Sleep never came.

Come daylight, the endless images that tortured her brain faded and disappeared. Wearily, she dressed and felt her way down the banister that descended the spiral stairs, shivering through the cold house, finally moving outside into the warmth of the summer morning. She continued across the gravel yard, stopping only when she reached the stables.

The groom greeted her with, 'Good morning, mam,' but, getting no reply and sensing her unease, saddled and helped her onto her horse without another word.

She rode, her senses dulled by lack of sleep, yet she felt them on fire. In the recesses of her troubled mind she believed her babies were listening and seeing through her the beauty of the countryside, each feature of oak, elm, beech and flower magnified; hearing the patter of tiny animals timidly scampering away as her horse approached, the tweet, squawk and coo of every birdcall amplified. This was her present to them: nature's beauty. It was their anniversary, after all, the anniversary of their death.

She rode on in a trance over the fields and through the woods. Hearing but not hearing. Seeing but not seeing. Her chestnut mare carried her unrestrained to the banks of the river, disturbing the nesting waterfowl amid the reeds, and leisurely stretched its neck to the water. She looked down at the sunlight playing on the ripples as the horse drank and she breathed a quiet sigh, imagining the splashes her boys would make throwing stones and skimming them across the river.

The visions vanished and her reverie was brought to a premature end. Over the ambling river's gurgling water, she heard the austere tones of the Peculiar Man.

'Here you are.'

She lifted her head; it felt so heavy. She gazed blearily upon the peculiar grey-haired man, her husband, astride his black horse.

The Peculiar Man appeared not to notice anything untoward about his wife and continued. 'Wondered where you were when you didn't appear for breakfast. Get in line now and you can accompany me while I ride.' Without waiting for a reply, he rode off along the riverbank.

Torn between his order and the images of her babies, muddled and confused, she obeyed meekly and followed.

The Peculiar Man cantered, following the course of the river for a while, then turned, spurring his mount across the open meadow and up a grassy hill. She trailed behind, her auburn hair hanging limp and lifeless. On the crest of the hill, which offered a good view over the surrounding land, the Peculiar Man brought his mount to a stop and waited. As she arrived alongside on her chestnut mare he stuck out his chin, surveying the expanse before him. As he spoke, he gestured with a sweeping arm.

'As you are aware, my dear, I own everything you see for miles around. No matter where you look in front, behind, to the sides, I own it all. All mine, my dear, all mine.' But his voice swiftly turned vile as with one reedy finger of his soft outstretched hand, he pointed into the distance towards stone-walled fields and a white-brick house with a few motley wooden buildings beside it and spat out the words: 'Except that. That is a cancer on my eyes, do you hear me? A cancer on my estate and a cancer I intend to cure!'

The farmland to which the Peculiar Man gestured had been given by one of his distant ancestors to a lowly commoner as reward for saving his son. The story was that the ancestor's son was born deformed. This in no way stopped the father loving the boy; in fact, the father idolised his son. On a winter's day they were riding together down by the river. With the season's rain and the melting snow running off the mountains, the river was ice cold, swollen and running fast. As father and son rode, the boy's horse stumbled and the child catapulted headlong into the water.

Neither father nor son could swim. The father was helpless, believing his son would drown, and he surely would have done if not for a passing stranger who dived into the swirling river. The father, watching from the bank, thought that both the man and boy would perish. The stranger struggled desperately through the raging water, swimming with all his might, and somehow managed to reach the boy and pull him back to shore. The father, overjoyed at having his son safe in his arms, thanked the stranger. He asked his name, to which the stranger replied, 'Marcus Bradshaw, my Lord.'

'Well, Mr Bradshaw, as reward for saving my son you will have

this land that you stand upon. I will have the deeds drawn up.'
Ever since then, the land had passed down from one generation
of Bradshaws to the next – although it must be said that the land
was of poor quality and of little worth to the lord.

The questionable quality of the land was no recompense to
the Peculiar Man, whose venom had no end. He continued to rant
and rage. 'How dare he give my land away to some peasant? His
brat should have been drowned at birth, not allowed to live and
breathe, tarnishing the family name with its disfigurement. Did
the fool not realise when the brat fell into the river that the current
would have swept it away, put it out of its misery and done us all a
favour? Then, I ask you, the fool goes and rewards the commoner
for risking his life and saving the child by giving him my land. *My*
land, do you hear me? *My* land! I would have tossed the deformed
creature back into the river, kept my foot on its head until I was
sure it'd breathed its last and had the interfering peasant whipped
for good measure.'

She heard his words but some more than others penetrated.
How dare he mention drowning little ones? How dare he mention
killing infants on today of all days, the anniversary of the twins'
death? For the very first time in their marriage, she turned her
back on her husband and rode down the hill, thoughts of the
ancestor and his son playing on her unsettled mind.

How brave of a passer-by to risk his own life to save a deformed
child. She would have given anything for such a man while she
laboured giving birth but there was no such man present that day
to come to her rescue, only her peculiar husband. She asked herself
how she had managed to get involved with this man, although
she already knew the answer. To her deep regret she had fallen
head over heels in love with him at their first introduction; she
had been mesmerised by his power, wealth and breeding. Naively
she had believed that only a great nobleman of intelligence and
upstanding morals could have accumulated such vast riches. How

innocent and foolish she was to have believed such things; the only excuse she had was that she was young and their courtship was far too brief.

She remembered their wedding: the cathedral, the red carpet, the marquees on the lawns of the manor and being oh so happy, truly believing he loved her. But she quickly realised that what love there was only ever came from her. From their very first meeting he played with her emotions and used her to satisfy his own selfish ends. To the Peculiar Man she was nothing more than a baby-making machine of the correct pedigree, an aristocratic womb, a highbrow depository for his seed, a fitting possession to produce him the son and heir he craved to bolster his manhood.

She left the Peculiar Man ranting but, seeing her riding down the hill, he spurred his own mount on and overtook her. A wife's place was behind her husband, not in front. He had his image to uphold, after all!

They continued over the meadows and she fell further behind. Up ahead, the Peculiar Man steered his horse through an open gate and into the lane leading back to the manor. She followed; as she reached the gate, and with her mind elsewhere, she failed to see the horse-drawn caravan coming along the lane. Only at the last second did she manage to stop.

Holding her mount steady while the horse passed, she couldn't help but notice the difference between the worn-out old animal and the bright and colourful caravan it was pulling. The caravan's sides were vivid green, with windows and dark crimson slatted shutters, the curved roof a golden yellow with a little black chimney sticking out on top. The sight of the gaily coloured wagon brought a weary smile to her sombre face.

The caravan drew level. The driver, a dark-haired gypsy, slouched with his legs dangling over the footboard. He leaned out and gave her a casual salute. She hesitated then nodded and, for a moment, could not help but envy the carefree life she imagined the gypsy must have as he travelled the countryside. Strange though, she had a fleeting recollection she may have seen the caravan and its driver somewhere before but she could not remember when or where; nor, as the caravan continued on its way and her melancholy returned, did she really care. The thought went out of her head as quickly as the slight smile on her face disappeared.

When they reached the ancestral home, the grooms saw to the horses. The Peculiar Man and his wife left the stables and crossed the gravel courtyard, entering the manor through the studded oak door with its large blacksmith's nails. They went their separate ways, the Peculiar Man to the library and his wife continuing along the cold marble hallway to the study.

Gently closing the study door, she crossed to an inlaid mahogany writing bureau in front of the French windows. Sitting down, she picked up a pen and started to write. Her hand was unsteady and the nib scrawled slowly across the paper, but the note was brief. When she finished she gently waved the paper, out of habit more than necessity. With the ink dry, she picked up an envelope and wrote her husband's name. She rose but, feeling dizzy, grabbed the bureau for support and steadied herself. Then, picking up the envelope, she left the room.

Crossing the marble hall, she entered the billiard room and turned the key, locking the door behind her. She placed the envelope on the green-baize table and made her way to the far side of the room and the gun racks mounted on the wall. On tiptoe, she reached up and lifted out a double-barrel shotgun. She broke open the gun and took out two cartridges from a box inside a cabinet under the racks. She loaded the gun, snapped it shut, then moved to the window.

She looked out over the garden. She saw the dainty French pansies, the drooping red-lipped tulips, the wild lavender, white tree roses framed in the background by the waxy green-leaved rhododendron bushes. For a brief moment she reflected on the few happy hours she had spent in the gardens amongst the flowers ... she would find happiness again soon.

She turned the shotgun upside down, putting the stock on the thick-pile carpet so the gun was upright, bent over, wrapped her mouth round both barrels of the gun, reached down and pressed the trigger. Brain and blood splattered the window.

The butler, Jarvis, heard the noise of the gun and came to investigate. He tried the door of the billiard room and found it locked. From his waistcoat pocket he pulled a silver chain to which a master key was attached. He tried the key in the door but the key on the other side prevented him from opening the lock.

Jarvis walked to the main door of the manor, let himself out and strode quickly to the outside of the billiard room. On seeing the bloodstained glass, he hurried to the window. Putting one hand above his eyes to shield the daylight's glare, he peered into the room. His stomach wrenched and he doubled up, gagging at the sight of her body.

It took a while for Jarvis to stop retching and pull himself together. Nauseous, he retraced his steps past the drooping tulips and into the manor house where he went to the library, knocked and entered. The Peculiar Man sat by the fireside, his legs crossed, browsing through the newspaper. Jarvis approached and said quietly into his ear, 'Sir, I have some rather distressing news.'

Jarvis and the Peculiar Man stood in the hallway, waiting for the estate handyman to jemmy open the billiard-room door. As the door sprang open, the Peculiar Man quickly put his arm out and blocked the handyman from entering.

'You may go now,' the Peculiar Man informed him. The handyman put the crowbar back inside his canvas tool bag, picked up the bag from the marble floor and left the manor by the back door through which he had arrived.

The Peculiar Man and the butler went into the billiard room; the Peculiar Man saw his wife's prostrate body and shouted at

Jarvis, 'Close the bloody door, man!' He added quickly, 'And get a chair and wedge it up against the door to make sure it stays shut.'

The Peculiar Man crossed the room; he saw the envelope on the billiard table, addressed in his wife's handwriting and, without breaking stride, snatched it up and put it in his trouser pocket. Looking down at his wife's body, his first thought was that it was a pity she hadn't done it earlier; that would have saved him a lot of trouble and unnecessary expense.

He turned to the butler standing by the door. 'You – and you alone, Jarvis – are to clean up this bloody mess. Anything you cannot clean, take out and burn. Once the room is in order, inform me and I will deal with the undertaker. You are not to say a word to anyone about this, do you understand? No one is to know what happened here. If anyone finds out there will be severe repercussions. Do I make myself clear? Now close the curtains man, and make sure this door stays shut.'

The butler nodded. The Peculiar Man removed the chair from the door and went back to the library.

The Peculiar Man picked up the newspaper to resume his reading but, as he sat down, he felt the envelope in his pocket. He pulled the bothersome thing out and removed the letter from inside.

I did not ask you for anything during our marriage so I beg of you now to grant my last request. Bury me with my boys so I may finally find peace and happiness together with them again. Your supplicant wife.

The Peculiar Man considered that she had done him a favour by doing away with herself; she was a possession that had not borne fruit. He would grant her wish, he thought benevolently. He crumpled up the letter, threw it into the fire and watched it burn.

Chapter 4

DOWNTRODDEN

THREE MEN, SHIRTSLEEVES rolled up above their elbows, hauled crates of milk along a concrete ramp and loaded them into horse-drawn carts. Each crate held twelve bottles of milk, most capped with silver foil but one or two with golden foils. The gold-foil bottles contained the thicker, creamier, more expensive milk. This, however, was the 1930s, the years of the Great Depression: few people could afford the cheap silver-top milk let alone purchase the gold.

Once a cart was loaded, a man in the dairy uniform of blue peaked cap and button-down long white coat flicked the reins, shouting, 'Move on.' The horse strained as it took up the load and pulled the cart across the smooth tarmac yard towards the open wooden gates at the far end. The wooden gates were light blue in colour; on each gate, a signwriter had painted the words in bold white letters, Wilkinson Dairy Ltd, and underneath, 'The Finest Milk in the Land'.

Once through the gates, the horses and carts came out onto the uneven cobbled streets where the milk bottles started to rattle. The din of the bottles in their crates, the clash of the horses' steel-shod hooves, echoed within the grimy terraced houses lining the streets, the racket stirring the dwellers from their night's uneasy rest.

Some of the occupants, who couldn't afford or had pawned

cherished timepieces, were grateful for the bottle-rattling, hoof-on-stone-cobble chorus. It was their wake-up call. On hearing the din, they dragged themselves from underneath the layers of ragged sheets, coats and anything else they used to keep warm. Splashing cold water over drowsy faces, men, women and children eligible to work scampered outside; even if they had food in their cupboards, they had no time to stop and eat. They were in a race along with countless others to be first in line outside any mill, shop or factory rumoured to be hiring labour.

Sadly there were other dwellers who, after months of desperately trying to find work, had lost all will and given up. Hearing the milk wagons, they simply rolled over in their beds, pulled the rags that covered them tighter and prayed it was all a bad dream. Feeling the pain of their empty stomachs, seeing their children's gaunt faces and 'the missus' giving up her meagre ration to pacify the kids was purgatory. Distraught and desperate, with nowhere to turn, many took their own lives to escape the misery rather than suffer further.

All the terraced streets looked the same and, in this time of mass unemployment, all reeked of hopelessness. The two-up two-down domiciles, often called cottages, were the furthest thing from a country cottage you could imagine. They did not have whitewashed walls with cute little bull-nose windows, thatched roofs, gardens of grass and pretty flowers where children could play. These were factory-workers' quarters built from red brick, stained with the filth of decades of industrial pollution. Rooftops were not covered with reeds but with grey slate infested with patches of fungal moss that thrived in the damp air. The houses did not have gardens but small yards with an outhouse, a closet-sized building, inside which there was a porcelain toilet – usually with no seat – and an iron hook with strips of old newspaper hanging from the wall.

The houses were all alike inside: a parlour at the front, a small room at the back that was the kitchen. A narrow passage ran from the front door to the kitchen; some folk called it a hallway. A steep staircase led up to a square landing and two bedrooms. The front of the terraces gave onto grey-slab pavements. Every week the women who lived in these 'cottages' opened the front door, got down on hands and knees and, with a bucket of water by their side and scrubbing brush in hand, worked away for all they were worth at the little bit of pavement immediately in front of their door. They spent ages trying to get the slabs clean and shiny; why was a mystery because they remained just as dull and dirty.

Chapter 5
WINDOWS HAVE EARS

THERE ARE NO such thing as secrets... especially in a house full of servants.

The handyman, when summoned, grabbed his tool bag from inside the work shed and made his way up to the manor house. As he went through the grounds, along the gravel pathways between the gardens, he passed the window of the billiard room. He saw the crimson-smeared panes of glass. He mentioned it to the young parlour maid as she let him in the back door; she mentioned it to the cook who, throughout the course of the day, told anyone and everyone who entered the kitchen until eventually, later in the evening, she managed to corner Jarvis alone and interrogate the poor man.

The cook, like many women, was adept at prising out information. The butler said very little, hardly anything at all really; nevertheless, from what little he did say and more from what he did not, the cook was shrewd enough to derive a conclusion, particularly when the Peculiar Man's wife failed to appear for lunch and dinner.

When the cook arrived home that night she told her husband, George, all about the day's events at the manor. He listened as usual, pretending a keen interest in what she had to say; he had learned very early on in his marriage that it paid to keep in her good books, especially when you needed to borrow a penny or two to nip down to the pub and buy a pint. Therefore, as his wife talked, he appeared to give her his full attention; he was desperate to get down to the Swan and Cemetery for a drink. He could tell from her voice that she was concerned about the Peculiar Man's wife and his eyebrows rose a tad at the mention of the bloodstained window; even so, he was more interested in getting down to the pub.

'Blood on the windows, you say. I'll tell you what, love, something sounds a bit fishy. You just make sure you lock the door when I go out. I'll not be stopping out long, mind you, after hearing that bit of news. I'll be back in a trice. Oh, by the way, you couldn't lend me a few pence so I can get a pint, could you, love?'

His wife shook her head as she looked in her brown bag for her purse. 'Honestly, I swear, George, sometimes I think you care more about that pub than you do me.' She handed him a shilling, saying, 'You just mind to get back here early. I'm telling you, something ain't right and I don't fancy being on my own for long tonight.'

'Right you are, love. I'll just have the one and be straight back.' And with that, he nipped sharpish out of the door and off down the street before she had a chance to say anything more.

The cook locked the door behind him. She was worried and hoped it was all just servants' gossip and silly rumour-mongering. She liked the Peculiar Man's wife and would not wish to see any harm come to her. In her opinion, the Peculiar Man's wife was a good woman; she had just gone a bit strange after losing the babies, that was all.

)(()(()(

The gypsy flicked back his dark hair from his eyes as he stood at the bar and ordered a whisky. He waited on his change before taking his drink over to a shadowy corner of the pub where he sat on a bench, alone in the crowded, smoke-filled room.

The gypsy pulled out a tin roughly the size of a packet of playing cards from inside his jacket pocket. He placed it on the beer-stained table, removed the lid and lifted out a small blue packet that lay on top of the tobacco. He pulled out a piece of gummed paper, sprinkled a fingertip of tobacco evenly along it, then rolled the paper between thumb and forefinger until it was evenly round. He brought the cylinder up to his mouth, licked the gummed edge and ran his thumb along the cigarette. He struck a match then stretched out, laying back his head; with eyes closed, he drew deeply on the cigarette while letting his ears grow accustomed to the humdrum chit-chat in the room.

His ears flitted from one conversation to the next, searching for any useful scrap of information. By the time he had finished his third cigarette he was satisfied there was nothing of interest to keep him here. He was leaning forward, lighting a final cigarette and deciding whether to have one more whisky for the road, when the cook's husband walked in.

George had to wait for a man smoking a pipe to pick up his drinks and move away before he managed to get up to the bar and be served. While the landlord pulled his pint, the pub door opened and in stepped one of George's regular drinking buddies. Seeing his friend, George waved him over and turned to the barman saying, 'Make that two pints now, will yer?' The proprietor nodded and took down another glass from off the shelf above the bar. As the landlord pulled the beer the cook's husband asked his pal, ''Ave you heard about the Peculiar Man's wife?'

Hearing this, the gypsy rose and slipped smartly out from between the table and the bench. With his cigarette dangling from his lip, he joined the two imbibers at the bar. He decided he would have that last whisky after all.

The moon shone full and the stars glimmered silvery-blue as the gypsy left the Swan and Cemetery but he did not notice the beauty of the night sky as he wandered back along the quiet lane to his caravan. The gypsy's mind was on something else: the death of the Peculiar Man's wife.

He reached the barren field where he'd camped and, without so much as a glance at his worn-out nag, he went inside, slumped down on the bed and lay there, hands clasped behind his head.

The Peculiar Man's wife is dead, is she, he thought. That changes things. I think I need to pay a call on his high and mighty before I move on. I'll give him a bit of time before I goes and sees him. Give him time to get over his grief. I wouldn't like to upset him, me being so kind and understanding.

He gave a quiet laugh, then rolling over with thoughts of the unfinished business ahead, he drifted off to sleep.

Chapter 6
A Very Nice Funeral

On the day of the funeral, the Peculiar Man came down to breakfast dressed in slippers and striped pyjamas over which he wore a crimson smoking jacket. He had slept soundly and was quite looking forward to the day. He expected a good turnout and the occasion would give him a chance to catch up with old chums and acquaintances. Now, however, he was ready for a bowl of fruit compote, his morning favourite. He believed the stewed fruit worked wonders for his digestive system and kept him regular. He would probably follow the fruit with some ham and eggs. After all, there was plenty of time to enjoy a leisurely breakfast before getting ready for the funeral.

Several silver serving dishes were set out on top of the mahogany sideboard. The one at the end, next to his daily paper, contained the fruit compote. In the absence of household staff, he helped himself to a large ladle of the steaming fruit, picked up his paper, sat down at the table and began to eat while scanning the news.

Opening the broadsheet, his attention focused immediately on a photograph of himself and his wife. The Peculiar Man, especially in these circumstances, couldn't help but notice how well she looked in the picture. She was smiling and simply radiating happiness. His expression contrasted starkly with hers.

He recognised the photograph, which was taken while they honeymooned in France, the Arc de Triomphe in the background. He shivered at the memory. She was a bitch in heat, fawning all over him, demanding; she just would not, and could not, keep her hands off him.

To the Peculiar Man, the full sexual act and experience of sharing emotionally was a very difficult one; he felt it was dirty and most degrading. He was an asexual man, aroused by neither female nor male company. His wealth, his manor, his land, meant everything to him and he loved them with an unbridled passion. He tolerated other people, put up with their company to a point, but could easily live without them. His possessions, however, he could not.

The Peculiar Man had seen and learnt from a very young age that displays of honesty, kindness, passion and sensuality didn't get you anywhere in life nor make you a real man; they counted for nothing. People respected you, bowed down and grovelled before you because of what you owned. Wealth was power, the absolute measure of a man, not displays of emotion; hadn't his father proved that?

As a boy, the Peculiar Man had seen how people toadied up to his father. Women fawned over him, commoners bowed, doffed their caps and curtsied in his presence. As a young boy growing up in the manor, he wondered why; he hated his father. He would lie awake at night in his room wondering why everyone looked up to his parent, showed him so much respect and could not see the monster that he was. Oh yes, his father was a monster all right, a dirty, disgusting monster!

He had witnessed his father beat his mother until the blood ran from her nose and her eyes blackened. He had seen him rolling around with the scullery maid in the barn, straw all over them, her drawers cast aside, her skirt raised above her waist. It was not just the scullery maid; she was only one of many. Servants came and went but never before his father had his way with them.

It did not seem to matter what sex they were: male or female, he hankered after both. The Peculiar Man had seen his father kneeling down in front of the butler. The boy was looking for his younger brother the first time he saw them, on his way down the stairs to find him, when he saw the pair of them in the marble hall. He crouched down, peering through the banister rails and watched his father on his knees, his head moving up and down between the butler's thighs.

After the butler finished moaning, his father looked up, caught his son watching and immediately pretended that he had lost a cufflink from his shirt on the floor. He called the boy down to help him look for it. Sheepishly, the child joined in the pretence. All three of them crawled on all fours across the marble floor until his father triumphantly declared he had found the cufflink. However, the Peculiar Man was not fooled by his father: he knew exactly what they had been doing.

Even outside in the grounds he had caught sight of his father's foulness, this time with one of the gardeners. The two of them at it under the hanging branches, the gardener's trousers round his ankles, pressed up against the trunk of the big old willow tree, his father sitting between his legs.

His father disgusted him. The Peculiar Man knew without doubt what a perverted monster his father was, yet people doffed their caps and curtsied to him; the boy could not understand why. Then one day the answer came to him: it was because his father was extremely rich, lived in a fancy house and surrounded himself with expensive things. As a young boy, the Peculiar Man vowed he would have people respect and grovel before him. From that day forward, money and possessions became his one and only true love.

It was a happy day for the Peculiar Man when his father died and he inherited the estates. He felt cleansed and free: free from the monster; free from the cloud of sordid debauchery that hung over him like a stink while his father lived. Now he could live his life the way he wanted, free from depravity. Free to amass an even bigger fortune. Free for the world to see what a great man he was – or so he thought.

As time went by, rumours came to the Peculiar Man's attention regarding his overly long bachelorhood. These he could not tolerate. He also realised that if anything happened to him there was no one he could truly trust to carry on and look after his money and cherished possessions. He could not leave his lovely things to any Thomas, Richard or Harold; it had to be someone special, someone he could mould and shape to understand their true value and the power they brought. He required a son and heir. The fact that he needed and did not have one gnawed at him like a feeding maggot, so he looked for a suitable womb and married its bearer.

The Peculiar Man looked down again at the photograph and shuddered. His honeymoon was one of the worst experiences of his life; he had performed to pacify the bitch only so she would keep her hands and lips to herself and out of the necessity to produce an heir.

He shuddered again at the thought and forcibly dismissed the whole experience from his mind; it would put him off his breakfast. He continued reading the newspaper and cheered up as he read: *Wife killed in freak accident while partaking in pheasant shoot.* All's well, he thought; my reputation is still untarnished.

That was all that really mattered to him.

The Peculiar Man put down his paper and went back to the row of silver dishes. He decided not to have the ham and eggs after all. He settled for a soft-boiled egg and, after tapping the top with a silver spoon and watching the yellow yolk ooze over the shell, he continued his breakfast. He scanned through the rest of the paper before retiring to his dressing room.

The undertaker and funeral cortège drew up alongside the main entrance promptly at eleven o'clock. The Peculiar Man went onto the terrace with Jarvis following, fiddling to open an umbrella because the rain had come on. The Peculiar Man stopped at the top of the stone stairway leading down to the carriages, one hand on the balustrade, as he inspected the assembly. Four identical polished carriages in black and gold livery lined up behind the hearse. Each carriage was pulled by a team of plumed black horses, adorned with black capes displaying the Peculiar Man's coat of arms embroidered in gold. The funeral carriage was distinguished from the other carriages only by its glass-panelled sides. His wife's coffin lay within, surrounded by wreaths of white lilies; her chestnut mare was tethered behind. Four footmen wearing tall black hats and long black tailcoats stood in front of the hearse. They would lead the procession, walking in sombre fashion, leaving the estate workers dressed in their Sunday best to bring up the rear.

The Peculiar Man looked at the hearse and recalled the last time he had seen his wife, in the billiard room, her head blown in two. He had never seen her look half so good, he thought and chuckled inwardly. Smiling at his own wit, having inspected the entourage and finding it satisfactory, he walked happily down the stairs with a thoroughly soaked Jarvis by his side holding the open umbrella.

At the bottom of the steps, a footman sprang to attention and opened the door of the carriage for the Peculiar Man.

Chapter 7
BRACKEN

ON THE WHITE-WALLED farm, life went on as usual.

Ned Bradshaw had noticed that Molly was a touch jittery for such a normally placid horse. She displayed all the signs that she would foal soon. With a shovel in one hand and a long wooden-handled yard brush in the other, he went to the barn and set about cleaning out a stall and laying down fresh straw. It was the last job on his long list of things to do that day. Finished, he lay the brush and shovel up against the wall of the barn and went inside to the farmhouse to clean up and have dinner with his wife and daughter.

After dinner, with the plates washed and put away, Ned strolled down to the horse's field to bring Molly nearer to the farmhouse and get her stabled in the barn. He was accompanied by his dark-haired daughter, Jess, who skipped along by his side. Ned wanted to keep a close eye on the horse. He knew from long experience that you could never be too sure how birthing would go and another horse round the place would be a valuable asset. He did not want to leave anything to chance.

Ned latched the white gate and, in the last of evening's grey light, he and Jess led Molly up to the barn and put her in the clean stall. No sooner had they got Molly inside and settled when she lay down, rolled onto her back and started to make a series of short, sharp whinnies. Ned knew he wouldn't be leaving the barn anytime soon. In the dim light, he went over to get the oil lamp hanging by the door.

Molly, her coat covered in sweat, managed to get back on her feet. She stood trembling, rasping harshly through flared nostrils. The lamp lit up the stall as a series of spasms ran down the mare's flanks and a pair of hooves emerged from her hindquarters. Molly let out another shrill squeal, panting heavily, and the foal's head followed quickly.

'Appears Molly's not one to keep us waiting,' said the farmer, hands in his trouser pockets, smiling down at his daughter. With a slurping whoosh, the rest of the foal slithered out and dropped onto the straw. 'My God, lass,' said Ned, 'that's one quick birth. One of fastest I've seen.' He pointed. ''Tis a stallion, see.'

With the lamplight reflecting off the wet embryonic fluid, the golden-brown coat of the new foal sparkled. Jess looked on wide-eyed at the newborn creature. Unable to contain herself, she whispered, 'He's lovely Dad. Look at his colour; it's the same as autumn bracken on the hills. And look, his mane and tail are jet black! He's beautiful, isn't he?'

'You're right there, lass. He's a sight to behold, no doubting that, and he'll be a blessing round the farm when he's older, by the looks of 'im.'

The foal began to move. Warily it lifted its neck slightly off the fresh straw then a little higher until, with head fully raised, it turned and slowly looked round. Jess thrilled as the foal's eyes rested on her but suddenly, quite unexpectedly, its head flopped to the ground with a thud. The animal lay still, deathly quiet.

Jess looked up anxiously at her father. 'Just give it a while and watch,' he said patiently.

As she watched, the foal pushed its front legs out and next thing it was up, teetering uncontrollably sideways, its spindly legs scrambling frantically, careering towards the rear partition of the stall. Jess screwed up her eyes, fearing the foal was about to crash into the wall, but at the very last second it found its feet using determination and willpower that she had not expected in such a newborn.

Jess realised she had been holding her breath the whole time but, with the foal standing motionless, steadying itself, she breathed out. Now Molly came over to lick her offspring tenderly and the newborn took another tentative step and began to suckle.

Watching the young stallion feed, a thought crossed Jess's mind. She said, 'What shall we call him, Dad?'

'There's a question for you now,' Ned replied. 'Looking at him, I'd say he's a strong 'un, there's no doubt about that. Did yer see his muscles ripple as he pushed hisself up off t'floor? When he's grown up he's going to be mighty strong, lass, tek my word for it. How's about we call 'im Hercules?'

'Hercules? I don't think so. He doesn't look like a Hercules to me, Dad.'

'What do you think of Goliath, then? 'Nuther good name for a horse, is that. Good strong name, is that.'

'Dad,' said Jess, 'I think there's more to this horse than muscles. Think of something else to call him.'

'Well, you think of some more names an' all, lass.'

Ned took one hand from his trouser pockets and rubbed his chin, mulling over what Jess had said: 'More to the horse than simply muscles.' As soon as the foal was born, Ned had cast his eyes over the animal checking to make sure it was okay and all was how it should be. When he looked at the foal's eyes, he saw they were open and noticed a peculiar brightness in them. He did not think anything about it at the time. Perhaps it was just the reflection of the light from the oil lamp or his imagination, but he also sensed there was more to this animal. What that something was he would not like to say; nor would he like to guess whether that something would turn out for better or worse.

Ned had not come across many animals that he would label bad. For sure there had been one or two but he knew that in most cases it was not the animal's fault; if it was difficult and unruly, it was usually the fault of its owner. Either they did not take the time to train the animal right, were cruel and unkind, or did not treat the animal with the respect that Mother Nature intended. He had wondered many times since at the stupidity of some people. He recalled seeing two small yappy dogs on a hot summer's day wearing thick, pink knitted cardigans. At the time he shook his head. No wonder they're making such a racket, he thought. Poor little things are boiling to death. Nature wouldn't have covered them in fur if she intended them to wear a flipping woolly pulley.

That being as it may, Ned had no doubt he would treat the little foal right but if it did turn out to be one of Mother Nature's bad 'uns, that would be a different kettle of fish!

Ned put his hand back in his pocket and, for his daughter's sake, hid any doubts he had about the young horse. Putting a wry smile on his face, he looked at Jess. 'You thought he were t'colour of wet bracken, did you, lass? Then how's about we call t'young 'un Bracken?'

'Bracken,' Jess considered. 'Bracken. I like that.'

With the young stallion's name decided, Ned and Jess remained in the barn watching the gentle interaction between mother and foal. Jess was pleased with the name Bracken and already had visions of bringing an apple down to the field and sitting on the white gate, calling out the horse's name and him galloping to her. She could see herself holding out her hand, Bracken nuzzling the apple off her palm, chomping away with his big horsey teeth.

Ned's thoughts were a bit different from his daughter's; he hoped the animal would turn out right. He could not afford the time or the trouble of having an unruly beast about the place.

Chapter 8
DEAD LUCKY

WITH HIS WIFE buried in the ground and the day's spectacle well and truly over, the Peculiar Man returned to his stately manor. Now comfortably settled in his favourite armchair, he pondered the day's events. All in all, he considered it had been a good day.

At last he was rid of that miscarrying woman. The funeral service had run on time and gone without a hitch; in addition, he had had a pleasant time meeting up with his old chums, many of whom had influential business connections. He had thoroughly enjoyed reminiscing about old times, not to mention them tipping him the wink on some interesting corporate information. He made a mental note of the engineering companies they had mentioned; over the next few days he would be sure to purchase sizable amounts of their shares prior to the news of their takeover becoming public.

Then, to top the day off, there was the young Miss Elora Rasstone.

As the Rasstones were old friends of his wife, he had observed protocol and invited them to her last public event, so to speak. The Peculiar Man never imagined their daughter would accompany them; when he had last seen her she was only a slip of a girl. Looking at her now, it was obvious she had done some growing up. Her black dress displayed her ample charms becomingly and her hair was tied up under a matching dainty bonnet.

After a brief tête-à-tête, the Peculiar Man realised that an extremely suitable filly to become his next wife was standing before him. The young Miss Elora ticked all the right boxes: attractive in a homely sort of way; pleasing deep brown eyes; long silky black hair and, from what he gathered from their exchange of words, she had little grey matter between the ears – a virtue in his eyes. Most importantly, she was of good breeding stock and had a fine pair of childbearing hips.

The young woman appeared to fit the bill admirably. After all, he was never going to love the creature, he just needed the use of her womb. He would still have to go through the bothersome nonsense of seeding her but perhaps she would fall in the family way quickly and that would be the end of such nonsense.

Overall, it had been a very pleasant funeral; it was just a shame there had been no let-up in the rain.

XXXX

The gypsy sat hunched at the front of the caravan, a black tarpaulin draped about him as the rain bounced off the caravan's yellow roof. As instructed on previous occasions, he waited until late at night before he came a-calling. The Peculiar Man had grieved long enough. It was now late and time to pay him a visit.

The gypsy eased the tarpaulin open far enough to roll a cigarette and smoke while he drove, thinking about how he would spend the money that was coming his way. He had smoked five cigarettes by the time he reached the manor; the fifth had burnt down to his fingertips. He took a last draw and flicked the stub out into the rain as he stopped the old horse and cast aside the wet tarpaulin.

Jarvis knocked on the drawing-room door. The Peculiar Man was sitting in his favourite armchair. 'Excuse me for troubling you at this time of night, sir, especially with you having had such a tiring and distressing day, but that character has turned up again.'

'Character?' said the Peculiar Man. 'What character? Stop talking in riddles, man. Speak the King's English.'

'You know, sir, that rather colourful fellow with the gaily painted wagon.'

'Ah,' said the Peculiar Man as he realised to whom Jarvis was referring. 'I see. Where is he now?'

'I've left him inside the servant's vestibule sir; it really is a most foul night.'

'Yes,' said the Peculiar Man, thinking. 'Quite right. Go and keep an eye on him and bring him through when I ring. I've got one or two matters to deal with before I see him.'

'Very good, sir.'

The Peculiar Man had a good idea what the gypsy wanted. He gave Jarvis a few minutes to return to the vestibule then got up and went through to the study. He went to the inlaid bureau in front of the French windows, pulled out the top drawer and felt underneath. His fingers touched a little ivory button. He pressed it and a box sprang out, revealing a cleverly concealed compartment. The box was stuffed with white fifty-pound notes.

The Peculiar Man took a handful of money and counted out a sum, laying it on top of the bureau. He was about to put the rest back in the box when he paused. He picked up the money again, counted it for a second time but this time he counted only half of the original amount. He put this in his trouser pocket and returned the rest to the box. He closed the compartment and returned to the drawing room. Seated in his armchair, he rang for the butler.

The gypsy and the butler sat on wooden stools in the vestibule. When the bell rang Jarvis rose, took hold of the gypsy's arm and said, 'He will see you now. Come with me.'

When they entered the room, the Peculiar Man told Jarvis to wait outside. As the door shut, the Peculiar Man got up. With his hand on the money in his pocket, he faced the gypsy and spoke in a high-handed manner. 'You will have come for your money, no doubt.' He withdrew his hand from his pocket, stepped forward, vigorously stuffed the white notes into the gypsy's top pocket and stepped back again.

The gypsy stared menacingly at the Peculiar Man then slowly removed the roll from his breast pocket. He counted out the notes one by one before lifting his head and scowling. 'This is only half the money. Where is the rest?'

'Correct,' replied the Peculiar Man. 'As I recall, our arrangement was that you supplied me with a little something. You haven't supplied me with that something and now I'm in a position where I don't require it any more. Therefore, the deal is off! So if I were you, I'd think myself awfully lucky that I was getting any recompense at all considering I hadn't done anything to earn it.'

The gypsy looked at the money. 'Humph,' he breathed. 'It will do.'

The Peculiar Man was taken aback by the gypsy's response; he had expected more fight from the grubby fellow and could not believe his good fortune. Not wishing to press his luck, he quickly went to the door and told Jarvis to see the gypsy off the premises. Then the Peculiar Man sat back down in his favourite armchair and rubbed his hands together.

Yes, this had been a good day, a very good day indeed.

Chapter 9
EASY TRAINED

BRACKEN HAD BEEN playing in the field long enough. He was weaned and independent of Molly now. The time had come to take the young horse in hand, to make a start and get him ready to earn his keep.

First things first: Ned knew he would have to get the horse used to the halter. He had bought one down at the farmers' market especially for the purpose and, as he strolled down to the white gate and the horses' field, he had it in his hand. He was uncertain how things would go. From the very beginning, he had been unsure about which category he should place Bracken in. Rightly or wrongly, he had earmarked the young stallion in the onerous group and, as he opened the gate, he was prepared for the worst.

Ned put the halter at his feet and called Molly over. Bracken came trailing along. With both horses by his side, Ned unbuckled and removed Molly's halter then slipped it back on and fastened it again. He repeated this exercise three times, each time making sure Bracken could see the harness did not hurt Molly and that she remained calm. After the third time of removing and refitting, Bracken stepped forward and started to sniff the leather straps. Not wanting to waste an opportunity, but realising he was chancing his arm, Ned started slowly and carefully placing the halter over Bracken's head, softly talking to the young horse all the while. He took his time getting it in place and once it was there he did not buckle the straps; he let the halter hang loose, all the time noting Bracken's behaviour.

Bracken seemed calm and at ease but Ned thought he'd best leave things as they were for a moment longer. Pretending to ignore Bracken, he turned his back on the young horse and gave his full attention to Molly, stroking and patting her flanks with an exaggerated show of affection. Seconds later, Bracken butted Ned lightly on the back. The young horse was jealous; he wanted Ned's attention.

Ned pushed Bracken away, pretending to ignore him again but there was no dissuading the animal. Tail swishing, he started nibbling Ned's ear. Ned brushed him aside again but the young horse was determined. Bracken pushed his head in between Ned and Molly and, nibbling and butting, manoeuvred Ned away so he had him all to himself.

Ned was smiling. He took hold of Bracken's halter and in a good-humoured but stern voice said, 'Is this what you're wanting? Is it, you young impatient animal, you.' He started to adjust the straps and tighten the halter buckles. When the halter was adjusted to a good fit, Bracken let out a neigh and cantered off across the field, seemingly happy with his new accessory.

Ned went back to Molly. 'Well, I think that's enough for today, old girl. Your son did well. We'll leave it on him for tonight and see how he goes tomorrow.' He gave her a final pat and rub on the muzzle before leaving both horses in the field. Closing the white gate securely behind him, he sauntered back up to the farmhouse.

Next morning, before Ned brought the cows in for milking, he returned to the white gate. Molly was grazing in the middle of the field and Bracken was down at the bottom. Ned, one foot resting on the gate, one eye on Bracken, called out, 'Molly'.

Molly stopped grazing and looked up; at the same time Ned saw Bracken stand rigid with his ears erect. Molly, her tail swishing, began to amble over; as she did, Bracken's ears fell back down and he broke into a gallop. He covered the ground rapidly to fall in line behind Molly.

With both horses at the gate, Ned reached up and patted Molly, gently running his hand along the length of her ears, stroking them and giving them a soft tug. As he expected, Bracken did not like Molly getting all his attention. Bracken pushed his head between them, forcing Molly to back away. Ned, laughing, firmly took hold of Bracken's halter and playfully shook it right and left, patting the horse with his other hand.

There was method in all that Ned did. He knew the young horse would be calmed by his gentle touch, and tugging and riving at the halter would enforce the knowledge that Bracken had nothing to fear. It also gave Ned a second chance to ensure it fitted correctly and required no further adjustment.

Fitting the halter was the first stage of readying the horse for training; it had gone well. The next step was to teach Bracken to respond to his name. Ned had enough work to do about the farm and could not afford to spend time calling to a horse. He knew fine well that this would happen quite naturally between Jess and Bracken. His real work with the horse would start in another couple of years when Bracken's young bones and joints had hardened. Therefore stage two, getting the horse used to his name, was down to Jess.

Jess was already spending more time than was good for her schooling watching, calling out and playing with the young horse. Now Bracken wore a halter, Jess could easily take hold of him and Ned knew his daughter would take every opportunity to lead the horse up to the barn and give him a good brush down. No doubt while she was doing it she would be whispering sweet nothings in the animal's ear: 'Good boy, Bracken, have your ears brushed now, Bracken. Now I'm going to brush your tail, Bracken. You make sure you stand still, Bracken,' and other such nonsense that young girls say to animals. It served the purpose of familiarising Bracken with his name and in no time at all the horse would come when he was called.

No, thought Ned. The horse has had enough of my time for the moment. I'll get down to the serious work of getting him fit for the wagon and the plough when he is good and ready.

Chapter 10
RABBITS ON THE RUN

JESS LOVED TO sit on the big white gate and watch Bracken. She found it hard to believe some of the things he got up to.

Often Jess would see Bracken down in the lower corner of the pasture. There was a rabbit warren under the hedgerow. She would watch as he poked his head down one of the rabbit holes, exploring, looking and sniffing. It was funny to see him standing patiently, ears pointed and erect, listening intently for the furry creatures. Sometimes a rabbit would pop its head out from a hole and Bracken would flinch slightly. Jess could tell he was getting ready then, just waiting for it to come all the way out. When a rabbit did emerge, he set off, chasing after it like a mad thing, going as fast as his young spindly legs would carry him. The rabbits evaded him easily, turning this way, darting that way, their big hind feet propelling them forward, hopping to the left and right, dodging Bracken and darting back down a hole. But things changed as Bracken matured.

Jess saw Bracken growing more subtle, more intelligent. The rabbits no longer had it all their own way. Bracken was faster too and seemed to have learnt the ways of his little hopping nemeses. Instead of the rabbits toying with Bracken and leading him a merry dance, Bracken now had the upper hand. He would stand, waiting for a rabbit to poke its head up. Without the slightest movement, so as not to scare the little creature, he would wait until it hopped some distance from the burrow. When the rabbit was far enough away, he would make his move, charging head down, keeping his body between the rabbit and hole, blocking off any means of escape and chasing it round and round the field.

Jess could tell Bracken was enjoying himself and, being a farmer's daughter, knew the value of these games; they were the natural way for young animals to learn, strengthen their muscles, quicken their pace and sharpen their intelligence. Jess was in no doubt whatsoever that Bracken was learning and learning quickly; he was an intelligent animal.

Jess also noticed that, for such a young animal, Bracken displayed a – she could not quite identify the word – a kind of honesty about him: a certain amount of pride would be the best way of describing it. Once Bracken had gained the upper hand with the rabbits, the game didn't end cruelly with him hurting or injuring them. No, Bracken was not a stupid, cruel animal, he was far too proud and – possibly the word Jess was searching for – noble to inflict mindless suffering on another creature. Jess loved him all the more for that.

Jess also saw how these games now ended on his terms. When the young stallion had had enough, considered that he had learnt something new, or had gained speed or recognised that the rabbit he was chasing was getting tired, he slowed down, stopped and allowed it to hop away un-menaced. It was as if the horse were saying, 'Look at me! I've beaten you; you helped me better myself. Thank you for the game, it was great fun.'

Going about the farm, Ned couldn't help but see Bracken and the games he played. Consequently, as time went by he lost the initial fear he had about the horse. Truth told, he was taking quite a liking to the young animal. Bracken made him laugh and who wouldn't laugh, seeing a young gangly creature so serious and committed to chasing rabbits about the place? It brought a smile to Ned's face just thinking about it.

Ned was a cautious type, however. He would not let his guard down entirely yet. After all, the horse was still young and Ned knew you should never trust an animal one hundred per cent, young, old or in between.

Animals get sick, tired and have their bad days, just like people. On those days they can be moody, irrational and bad-tempered, just like people. Unlike animals, however, people can tell you when they are not feeling well so you have fair warning; animals cannot.

When dealing with any animal you should always err on the side of caution – leastways that was Ned's philosophy.

Chapter 11
DEAD OR ALIVE ON THE FARM

FOR GENERATIONS THE farm had passed down from father to son. One day it would all be Ned's but he was in no real hurry for that day to come.

Ned was born on the farm. He worked the land alongside his father and mother until one day his father, Nathanial, had come home and told him he had enlisted and was going off to fight in the war, leaving Ned, then in his teenage years, and his mother to look after the farm.

Ned and his mother laboured away while his dad was away at war then one day a postman arrived and handed over a telegram; Nathanial Bradshaw had been killed in action.

At the outbreak of The Great War, Marshal Sir Herbert Kitchener, the British War Secretary, called for volunteers to join the armed forces. Nathanial was a thinking man and he did not volunteer at the time. He was fond of quoting though, particularly after a few pints on a Saturday night down in the Swan and Cemetery: 'All it takes for evil to prosper is for good men to do nothing,' so it was surprising he did not enlist straight away. Having said that, all the leading politicians and great generals agreed that it would only be a matter of weeks, at the most a few months, before the war was over. Nathanial reasoned that as an untrained soldier he would be more of a hindrance than a help in that space of time. But as the weeks passed, it became clear that the war would continue for some considerable time; not serving his country began to pray upon Nathanial's mind.

In July 1915, when Lord Kitchener made a second ardent recruitment speech, Nathanial joined the armed services. On no account, though, would he let his son enlist, explaining to Ned that it was his duty to stay at home and run the farm. 'Your mum can't run this 'ere place on her own, lad, and there's plenty of time for you yet to get some excitement in your life. Besides, you've got your young lady, Christine, to think about now and she wouldn't be too pleased with me if I let owt happen to you, would she?'

Nathanial Bradshaw joined the infantry together with his best friend Bert Hartley and several other local men. He survived the rigours of the war for nearly two years then, in the Third Battle of Ypres also known as Passchendaele, he was killed during a mustard gas* attack while helping a senior officer.

A long time after they received the telegram from the War Office, a postman came to the farm and delivered a small package. Inside was a medal awarded to Nathanial for courage above and beyond the call of duty. That day Ned took himself off to the barn, sat down on a bale of straw and, head in hands, cried as he had never cried before as the realisation finally hit home that he would never see his father, the man he loved and looked up to, again.

Fortunately, during this time Ned had Christine's love to comfort and console him. Ned had never known anyone quite like Christine, with her long black hair and creamy skin. She was like an angel when he needed one most and she seemed to understand him better than he understood himself. Not long after receiving his father's medal, Ned proposed to her.

---

* The Germans made full use of mustard gas during the Battle of Passchendaele. By any standard, the battle was a calamity for the British with some 310,000 soldiers killed, wounded or captured.

The couple had their wedding in the local church and the reception in the church hall with a buffet of sandwiches and fancy cakes. After the ceremony, Christine moved into the farmhouse with Ned and his mother. There was no honeymoon; they couldn't afford one.

Three years later, Christine gave birth to Jess. Her arrival was a truly happy day for all of them. Ned only wished his father were alive to see it.

Ned's mother loved Christine like the daughter she had never had and simply idolised little baby Jess. It was particularly hard for her, as the years passed and age took its toll, when she knew that it was time for her to leave and let the three of them get on with running the farm on their own. Age had caught up with her: her old bones were weary and could no longer manage the hard manual labour and the long hours. She knew she was becoming more of a burden than a help to her son and daughter-in-law.

Sitting round the kitchen table one evening, she said, 'It's about time now for me to put meself out to grass. I've gone and rented a little cottage at edge of town and got a little part-time job. I'll be comfortable down there and besides, it's about time you, Christine and Jess had entire run of place to yourself. I'd appreciate if you could help move me in.'

Ned looked up from his plate at his mother. He knew what she meant; he had seen her struggle these last months and many a time had stopped what he was doing and gone to help her. He knew it was time she took things a little easier and enjoyed the peace of her own company without having to consider others all day long. Nevertheless, it would be a sad time for them all when she left.

'No need to ask me, Mother. Of course we'll help you move but we're all going to miss you so much.' With his head down over his plate, Ned cut up a potato and stuffed it into his mouth so no one could see the tear in his eye.

Ned's mother signed the farm over to her son and, when the time came, Ned helped her to pack her belongings, loaded them onto the wagon and moved her into the small cottage. As Jess went round exploring the rooms of her granny's new home, Christine helped the old woman arrange her things and settle in.

The cottage was handy for Ned's mother. It was not far from the farm and fairly close to Wilkinson's Dairy where she had managed, through the help of one of Christine's friends, to get a small, undemanding job. The work would stop her getting bored and bring in a little money, enough to keep the wolf from the door. The cottage was also opposite the village pub, the Swan and Cemetery, and it comforted her to remember how much her dearly beloved husband used to enjoy coming down for a drink and sharing a joke or two with his friends. She still thought about Nathanial daily and missed him greatly.

Chapter 12
KNOCKED OVER

ON A SATURDAY morning Christine usually wanted Ned to take her into town to stock up on the weekly goods and to take the opportunity of going into some of the fancy dress shops to look at the latest fashions and fripperies. Ned did not mind the grocery shopping, he saw that as being essential, but he could never understand why someone would want to go into these overpriced places with all their frilly wear that the likes of them would never be able to afford. He considered it a waste of time, time he could spend doing something more productive. However, he put up with it for Christine's sake as she seemed to enjoy that type of thing and it appeared to make her happy. God only knows why, he thought; women are strange creatures.

For some reason, Christine didn't need to go into town this particular Saturday and Ned, having milked the cows and done most of the jobs about the farm, decided he would take advantage and have a bit of a lazy day for a change.

After lunch, he and Christine went for a leisurely stroll about the farm. They were chatting about this and that, stopping every now and then to look over the fields and the crops. They reached a field full of young cauliflowers, next to the field where they kept the horses. Ned picked up a cauliflower leaf. He was turning it over to have a quick check for pests, disease and what have you when all of a sudden, a sharp squeal shattered their peace.

Ned turned to the source of the noise, quickly looking over the hedge separating the two fields. He saw Bracken, rampant, head held high, eyes glaring. The next second, the horse was charging, flying over the turf. Ned glanced in the direction he was heading and caught sight of a postman entering the lane on his bicycle. Oh, God no, he thought. Aloud he said, 'That daft horse is going to jump t'hedge and attack t'postman. I knew it! I should 'ave listened to myself. That horse is going to be t'ruin of us.' He broke into a run.

Bracken looked like a demon, his black mane lashing against his back, his dark tail arrow straight, legs a-blur as he stormed over the field towards the postman. The poor postman heard Bracken before he saw him. He turned round at the noise and saw the rampaging horse bearing down upon him; fear gripped him. In his panic his hands froze, his legs refused to work. He lost control of his bicycle: the front wheel began to wobble, he fell off and the bicycle landed on top of him. The postman waited underneath it, waited with baited breath, listening to the pounding hooves come closer and closer, expecting the horse to fly over the hedge and land on him at any second.

Bracken hurtled toward the hedgerow. The postman shut his eyes tight, fearing the worst. Bracken charged on, the sound of his hooves a thumping military tattoo in the postman's ears.

Suddenly the muscles in Bracken's forelegs stiffened. His legs remained straight out in front of him, digging into the soft earth; his hindquarters swung round parallel to the hedgerow and he came to an abrupt halt. Then he leant calmly over the hedge, stretched his neck down and looked the petrified postman in the face.

It had all gone quiet. The worst hadn't happened. The postman opened one eye a fraction and peeked out, only to see Bracken peering straight back down at him. The postman quickly shut his eyes again, screwing them up tight. Bracken bent closer still; the postman could feel the horse's breath on his cheeks. The postman slowly opened his eyes once more and this time kept them open because instantly he was lost in Bracken's eyes, the glowing orbs so close to him. They were sparkling diamonds, burning fires, leaping flames of raw power but the flames were controlled, calm, measured; and behind the flames, in the inner depths, there was something else – a shimmering aura of spiralling, interweaving, ever-changing colours; the vibrant hues of strength, the soft shades of feeling and the intense bright tones of intelligence. The postman was so mesmerised that he could hardly bring himself to look away but when Bracken blinked, somehow he did.

Little by little the postman began to move, crawling out from underneath the bicycle. He got to his feet warily, lifted the bicycle and placed it slowly between himself, the hedgerow and the horse, using it as a kind of shield. His muscles quivering, incapable of riding, he began to walk tentatively towards the farmhouse, wheeling his bicycle. On the other side of the hedgerow Bracken's gaze never faltered as he kept pace alongside.

The postman gingerly made his way up the lane that curved away at the white gate and ran up to the farmhouse. Here he started to put some distance between himself and the horse as Bracken stopped and stood resolute, watching him go on up to the house and knock on the door.

As the postman took hold of the big brass doorknocker, he glanced behind. From here, seeing the horse standing in the field, he felt a whole lot safer; but as he looked towards Bracken, head held high, proud, he had to admit the animal had put the fear of death into him. Despite that, the horse was a truly fine sight, an awesome animal. As he knocked again on the door, the postman was thankful he had come across the horse when it was still young and not fully grown. He'd hate to be on the wrong end of it when it was.

As he waited for someone to answer, the postman swung the Royal Mail satchel from his shoulder and rummaged round inside. He pulled out two letters addressed to Mr N Bradshaw just as Jess opened the door. She was just about to say hello when she noticed her mum and dad scurrying up the lane.

Dad and Mum rushing round, what's going on? she wondered. Dad never rushes if he can help it and Mum certainly does not. Puzzled, Jess took the letters from the postman.

Ned reached the farmhouse, breathing heavily. He bent over, leaning with one hand on the door lintel, and panted, 'You all right? Don't know what came over the crazy young animal, charging at you like that.'

'I'm fine, no damage done 'cept to me pride, that's all. I durst tell you though, that's one hell of a spirited beast you've got there. Begging your pardon, ladies,' the postman replied tipping the peak of his cap. 'Didn't mind to use any profundity tha knows but that horse of yours, particularly for a young 'un, didn't half give me a scare. Fell off me bike, I did.'

'We know, we both saw. Are you all right? Would you like to come in for a sit down and a cup of tea?' Christine enquired.

'Yes,' said Ned. 'Come in and 'ave a cuppa and make sure you're all right.'

'No, no,' said the postman. 'Very kind of you to be concerned but as I said, no harm done. I've suffered worse from some of t'dogs on my round, I can tell you. Some vicious hounds out there with sharp teeth and I've got scars to prove it. Young stallion, is it?'

'Yes,' Ned answered.

'Ah, well, that says it all then,' said the postman, straddling his bicycle and leaving Ned, Christine and Jess wondering just what it did actually say. With a final 'Must be off, got a busy round to finish today, tha knows,' the postman peddled back down the farm lane no worse for wear but mindful to ride that bit faster as he got to the horses' field with Bracken still standing defiantly by the white gate.

'Mum, Dad, what was all that about?' asked Jess.

'Let's get inside and have a sit down so I can catch my breath,' said Ned. 'We'll tell you over a nice cuppa tea your mum's going to brew, ain't that reet, love?'

Christine needed a sit down as much as Ned did; nevertheless she went and put the kettle on.

Chapter 13
CALL FOR THE DOCTOR

AFTER THE INCIDENT with the postman, Ned's anxieties returned. Ned knew horses were by nature nervous animals; they had an inbuilt fright and flight response when faced with anything remotely intimidating. They certainly did not go round charging postmen on bicycles. Having witnessed this display, Ned knew for sure Bracken was not quite your normal horse.

Bracken never charged anyone entering and coming up the farm lane again. It was as if he had sensed the fear in the cowering man lying under the bicycle, had established his authority and spelt out the message: *As young as I am, do not think about messing with me. If you do, you do so at your peril.* Bracken had shown who was dominant and, having proved his dominance, two-legged creatures would never pose a threat to him again.

In the natural world of animals, this would probably have been right enough. Man however, has removed himself in many ways from the natural world and its inherent codes; man should never be trusted. Still, having shown his dominance, Bracken was not going to fritter away his energy on charging people coming up the lane.

However, he did charge again.

It was the middle of the night. Ned and Christine were fast asleep. All of a sudden, a moaning pierced the quiet of the house.

Bleary eyed, they stared at each other, sleepily trying to work out what the noise was. The moaning continued to puncture the silence. 'It's Jess,' said Christine, reaching out abruptly and putting her hand on Ned's chest.

They scrambled out of bed and hurried to Jess's room. Christine went straight to her daughter as Ned lit the bedside lamp. Jess lay covered in perspiration, her face bright red.

'Ned, go soak a towel in cold water and fetch the thermometer from the bathroom cabinet. Quickly,' Christine ordered.

Ned rushed to the bathroom, grabbed a towel and put it under the tap. As the water ran, he found the thermometer by the lotions and other medicines in the cabinet.

Christine wiped Jess's face and placed the folded towel over her daughter's forehead. She took the thermometer from Ned, shook it to ensure the mercury was down in the bottom of the bulb, and placed it under Jess's tongue. Christine sat on the side of the bed, mopping her daughter's feverish brow, waiting for the thermometer to register. Jess's temperature was very high.

Christine looked up at Ned, her voice full of concern. 'Ned, she's burning up. I think you need to go and fetch the doctor. Now!'

He didn't need telling twice. Ned rushed into their bedroom, hurriedly put on his trousers and raced down the stairs. At the bottom, he grabbed his jacket from the coat rack by the front door, slipped on his boots and rushed outside down the lane to the white gate, buttoning his jacket as he went.

Bracken, grazing in the field, heard the farmhouse door open and close. He watched as Ned came down the lane shouting, 'Molly, Molly, Molly'.

Molly trotted over to the white gate and was there as Ned unlatched it. He took hold of her halter and led her quickly to the barn. He threw a saddle over her, tightened it and rode off swiftly down the lane. Bracken watched as they turned onto the road and disappeared out of sight.

Some time later that night Bracken was lapping water from the old bathtub at the top of the field up near the white gate when he heard a strange noise. He stopped drinking; his head lifted and his ears pricked as the noise grew steadily louder. Unsure, his ears stiffened and his nostrils flared as two yellow beams of light appeared up the lane. This was something Bracken had never seen or heard before: a motorised vehicle.

Bracken charged at the oncoming car.

He thundered across the pasture to the hedgerow dividing the field and the lane. Yet again he stopped short of jumping the hedge but, unlike the postman, the little black Austin didn't stop and it kept moving up the lane. Bracken gave chase.

Concentrating, his eyes fixed firmly on the dark road ahead, the doctor drove on towards the farmhouse. He was unaware of the horse running alongside his car on the other side of the hedge. At the white gate, the doctor followed the lane on up to the farmhouse. As the car hadn't stopped, neither did Bracken; he reached the white gate and, in one bound, leapt over it and continued galloping after the car.

The doctor parked his Austin in the farmyard in front of the house, switched off the engine and grabbed his medical bag from the passenger seat. He opened the car door; as soon as he stepped out he heard Bracken's pounding hoofs and caught sight of the horse thundering towards him. Bracken was petrifying: ears folded back; lips drawn; white teeth exposed and gleaming in the darkness. For a moment the doctor froze.

Bracken reached the back of the car. Seeing the two-legged creature, he jarred to a stop and reared. Two-legged creatures were not to be feared. His front legs landed on the yard with a crash, sparks flying from his steel-shod hooves. He stood, neck stretched, staring straight into the doctor's eyes. The doctor did not wait for a second opportunity. With the horse stationary, he bolted for the farmhouse door, praying aloud as he sprinted: 'Please God, let the door be open.' He thanked God under his breath when he found that it was. He charged through the door, slamming it shut behind him and leaning his back against it. He stood catching his breath. When he'd recovered somewhat, he called out, 'Anyone home?'

Christine shouted down, 'Upstairs doctor.'

Outside Bracken took his time, slowly walking round the car, stopping and sniffing. He did not like its oily smell or the black sooty exhaust pipe but other than that, he could sense no danger or threat. He smelt the rubber tyres one last time then turned and looked at the farmhouse door before calmly trotting back down the lane to stand patiently by the white gate.

Ned had ridden into town, knocked and woken the doctor. He'd fidgeted in the surgery until the doctor was ready and had gathered up his medical bag. When the doctor set off in his little black Austin, Ned hurried as best he could back to Jess and Christine but he knew he could not go as fast as he wanted. He had ridden Molly overly hard and, for the sake of the horse, would have to take things easy on the way home.

Eventually Ned reached the farm. As he rode up the lane he was surprised to see Bracken outside the field, standing by the gate. He wondered how he'd got out but he was far too concerned about his daughter to do anything about the horse at that moment. He would put him back in the field later. Now all he wanted to do was get inside and see Jess.

Ned rode on up to the farmhouse. Dismounting and leaving Molly loose in the yard, he hurried in.

He took the stairs two at a time and went into the bedroom. The doctor had finished examining Jess and was speaking to Christine. 'I can't be sure at this stage but her initial symptoms suggest she has pulmonary tuberculosis.'

Christine turned to Ned as he came through the door. Seeing the perplexed and anxious look she gave her husband, the doctor

explained. 'You may know the illness by the name, consumption*'
Both their expressions changed to dread.

'Now all is not lost,' the doctor continued. 'The medical profession has made major strides in combating the disease and we have a few things working in our favour. Jess is young and fit and couldn't be in a better place. Here on the farm she will get plenty of fresh air, which is essential for her recovery, so try not to be too alarmed.'

Ned and Christine were too shocked to reply.

'I will be back tomorrow to re-examine Jess. I'll bring along some additional equipment to confirm my diagnosis. If I'm proved right, I will carry out a small procedure that will hopefully aid her recovery. In the meantime, apply cold compresses to keep her temperature down and open the window fully.'

Having done all he could for the time being, the doctor picked up his bag. Ned took this as a sign that the doctor was about to leave and, managing to find his voice, thanked him for coming and said he would show him out.

In the limestone hallway at the bottom of the stairs, the doctor paused and turned to Ned. 'By the way, when I got here tonight I was met by a rather angry horse. It frightened me half to death. I just managed to avoid it and get inside before it did me a serious mischief. I see it's still at large.' He pointed towards the white gate. 'I'd be grateful if you could make sure it doesn't attack me again or do any damage to the car as I drive back down.'

Ned looked past the doctor and saw Bracken. He shook his head. 'He won't be a problem, doctor. You get in your car and I'll go down and make sure he doesn't get up to any nonsense.'

The doctor waited in his car, looking out of the back window until Ned took hold of Bracken and waved to the doctor that

---

* Prior to 1948 and the introduction of the antibiotic streptomycin, the disease tuberculosis was more commonly known as consumption and had a high death rate among those infected.

everything was okay. The doctor started the engine and drove away from the farm. As his car passed, Ned whispered softly into Bracken's ear, 'Now young 'un, I think I have enough problems to be going on with without having to worry about the likes of you. So think on – you be good, eh.'

Bracken whinnied back in response and Ned took it as a sign the horse understood. He put the horse back in the field, latched the gate and went up to the yard to see to Molly before going back inside and up the stairs to be with Jess and Christine.

Next morning Bracken's ears pricked up as he heard the Austin's engine tootle up the road. His muscles tensed, ready to charge, but he didn't. Instead he cantered up to the top of the field and, with head held high, he stood by the white gate and watched the doctor's black car come up the lane. Bracken continued to watch as the doctor got out, walked up to the farmhouse, took hold of the brass knocker and rapped on the door. Christine opened the door, looking worried and worn out, and let him in.

Ned heard the doctor's car too. He took his fingers and thumbs off the cow's udder, got up off the milking stool and appeared moments later from the cow shed. There were more important things he had to attend to; he would finish the milking later. As he hurried across the yard to the house he caught sight of Bracken by the gate. Anxious as Ned was to hear what the doctor had to say, he found time to shout down to the horse, 'Good lad, keep it up, no nonsense, you mind.' Then he reached the farmhouse door and went up to Jess's bedroom.

The three adults stood round the bed looking down on Jess as the doctor confirmed she had pulmonary tuberculosis. The doctor's diagnosis hit Ned like a sledgehammer. He felt faint and sick and his eyes rolled round in his head. He realised Christine must be feeling the same and he put his arm round her. She was thankful for his tenderness.

The doctor gave them a private moment, turning away and

glancing through the open window at the view over the fields of the river and the distant hills. He couldn't help but think how much nicer life must be here as opposed to the declining conditions in the towns.

He averted his gaze from the window and returned his attention to Ned and Christine. 'If you recall, yesterday I mentioned that I may have to carry out a small procedure to aid Jess's recovery,' he reminded them. 'Now please don't be alarmed, it really is very straightforward, but it sounds a bit worse than it is. I have some equipment in the car that will let me inject air into Jess's chest cavity. This will make the infected lung collapse. In this state, the lung will be at rest and better able to heal. Jess's body will absorb air over time so I will have to repeat the procedure on a weekly basis to ensure the lung stays at rest. Do I make myself clear? Do you understand what I am going to do and have you anything to ask before I start?'

Ned and Christine stood, numbly shaking their heads. Both had grown up hearing 'The doctor knows best', so they asked no questions.

'Good,' the doctor continued. 'If you have nothing to ask me, could I have your help for a moment? Christine, if you could get me some clean blankets, towels and boiling water, I'd like to clean the area around Jess to reduce the risk of germs and infection. Ned, if you come with me I've got a few things in the boot of the car, some cylinders and fancy gadgetry that I'll need your help to carry.'

Christine went downstairs into the kitchen, filled pans with water and set them on the stove as the two men went out to the doctor's car. She felt sick and useless. Her poor daughter. What could she do? As she climbed the stairs with the towels and water, a grim determination came over her. She was dammed if she would fall apart like some weak woman and be of no use to man or beast. Her daughter was ill and needed her and she would do

71

everything she could to help her get better … even if it was only boiling water and fetching towels.

The doctor wiped around the room. He rolled Jess over, placed a clean blanket underneath her and rolled her onto her back again. He cleared the bedside table of her night lamp and book, then placed a clean towel on top and laid out his medical instruments. Picking up one of the instruments, he bent over Jess and made a small puncture in her skin just above her left lung. As he worked he explained what he was doing to Ned and Christine.

'I'm making a small incision. Now I'm inserting a tube and I'll inject air into her pleural cavity. This will cause the lung to deflate and help it rest and recover. As I said, it really is quite a simple procedure.' As the doctor worked, he watched the gauges carefully as he injected the air.

When he had finished, he turned to Ned and Christine. 'That's it, all done. All we can do now is let her rest and make sure she gets plenty of fresh air. Keep the window wide open and in time – and I'm talking months here rather than days or weeks – hopefully she'll mend.'

Ned and Christine were more than relieved that the operation was over; nevertheless, they both realised the gravity of the doctor's last sentence: 'hopefully she'll mend.' They knew that the outcome for Jess was far from certain and over the coming days and nights their daughter would fight for her life.

As Ned showed the doctor out, the doctor mentioned Bracken and broached a delicate subject. 'I'm glad to see you've got the animal under control, Ned. I can tell you, it didn't half give me a scare last night. If I was a betting man, I wouldn't have put money,' emphasising the word 'money', 'on reaching the door and getting inside before it got me. What do you think made the horse stop?'

Ned took the hint; the doctor was a gentleman and he had purposely but discreetly brought the word 'money' into the conversation.

The doctor hadn't wanted to embarrass Ned by coming out and asking directly for his fee. He knew these were hard times but nevertheless, he still needed paying for his services; he had to put food on the table and provide for his own family. Ned appreciated the doctor's tact.

He continued the charade, pretending not to notice the doctor's reference, and replied, 'That horse, that's young Bracken, that is. Came out of old Molly, well over a year ago now, I should think. That reminds me, he's comin' of an age now when he ought to be doin' a bit more than playing about in field and scaring folk. I'll 'ave to get me skates on an' start getting him into shape and used to doing a bit of work round the place.'

'He looks to be a fine, strong animal, Ned.'

'Oh he is that, doctor. But at same time he can be a might peculiar. Funny animal to work out. Mind you, our Jess don't think so. Can't say anything bad about t'horse in front of Jess. She thinks he's special. There when he was born, she was. Talking about Jess,' said Ned, bringing the conversation round to the real topic, 'how much do I owe you?'

The doctor told Ned his fee. 'Right,' said Ned. 'Okay if I pay you part in cash and makes up the rest with a couple of birds? I've got a couple of plump hens I've just plucked all ready for the pot and I'll throw in some fresh eggs an' all.'

'That would do nicely,' replied the doctor. 'I'm partial to a bit of chicken.*'

Ned went off to get the hens and gather some eggs while the doctor waited in the little Austin with the front door open. The doctor saw plenty of folk and knew that most of them round these parts, as honest and hardworking as they were, could not afford lengthy doctor's visits – or even short ones for that matter. A one-

---

* The NHS did not come into being until introduced by Lord Bevan in 1948. Up to then it was customary to pay the local doctor either in cash or kind or a mixture of both.

off yearly visit to the doctor was as much as most could manage.

Ned came back and handed over the two plucked birds and a brown paper bag of fresh-laid eggs. 'Thanks Ned, these will go down lovely with a few new potatoes and cauliflower. I'll drop by again tomorrow to see how Jess is getting on, and more than likely for the next several days.'

Ned noted the doctor's tactfulness once again. Tomorrow he would have a sack full of potatoes and a few cauliflowers ready and cleaned to hand to the doctor, together with the few coins he could manage.

The doctor drove off and Ned went back up to Christine and Jess. Christine stood up when he came into the room, threw her arms round him and burst into tears.

'Now, now,' said Ned. 'What's all this?' He knew that Christine had been up most of the night, emotional and upset. 'Now, now,' he said again, trying his best to think of words to comfort her. 'I know things don't look too good at the minute but that doctor's no fool. He's a good man, he is. You saw how steady he was when he saw to Jess and you heard him say Jess was young and strong. With all this fresh air we have up here, she'll be right as rain, you'll see. Now, hush now, hush.'

Christine's sobbing eased. She lifted her head from Ned's shoulder, looking at him closely as she held his face between her hands. 'You think so, Ned? You think so?'

'Of course I do. Now dry your eyes.' Christine withdrew a small white handkerchief from her cardigan sleeve. As she wiped her eyes Ned added, 'Jess's got the same wild spirit and fight as that young stallion out there. That's why she loves the horse so much; two of a kind they are. She won't let some bug beat her, I can tell you that. You've been up all night, it's sleep you need, love. Once you've had a bit of shuteye, you'll feel better. Off you go and have a good lie down while I sit with Jess.'

As Christine went off to their bedroom, Ned looked at his

daughter. He had told Christine that Jess would be all right but in all honesty he didn't know what to think. He was praying and willing the outcome would be good but he knew consumption was serious. One thing he was certain of, though: it was better for everyone's sake to keep positive rather than think the worst. Going round gloomy and depressed was not going to help anyone.

For the next few days, the doctor called round each morning. Hearing his little black car, Bracken trotted over to the white gate to wait and watch. The doctor always parked in the same spot, directly in front of the farmhouse door. After pulling on the handbrake, he would get his bag, stride over to the farmhouse and rap on the door with the big brass knocker. Ned or Christine came to the door or sometimes Ned's mother; she went up to the farm whenever she could to lend a hand. With all Christine's time spent attending to Jess, the old woman knew how hard it must be for Ned having a sick child to think about and running the farm on his own.

After working all day, Ned came in off the fields, had a quick wash in the kitchen sink and went straight upstairs to see Jess. He had carried a green armchair from the downstairs parlour up to her bedroom; it was more comfortable for Christine as she maintained her vigil. As the days passed and Jess's condition improved slightly, Ned often lifted Jess out of bed into the chair to give her some respite from constantly lying down. If Jess was awake, he carried her to the armchair, wrapped the blankets off the bed round her so she was nice and cosy, then sat on the bed and told her all about his day. He told her how the crops were growing, what he was thinking of planting next year, how many eggs he had collected and which hens were laying and which were not. He told her which animals were sick, which were with calf or had young but, no matter what he said, Jess only showed any real interest when he mentioned Bracken.

She would try to sit up but, not having the strength, lay back in the chair. Wheezing, she asked, 'How is Bracken? Huh, huh, hu, he…' stopping mid-sentence as she struggled for breath '… doing? When are you going to teach, hu, huh huh … him to pull the wagon … huh, huh, huh, huh … and plough?' she laboured.

'Now Jess, me girl, it'll be quite a while before young Bracken pulls anything, let alone a plough. You 'ave to take it slowly with young animals. Can't rush 'em or you'd fear 'em, see, and put 'em off right from start. And that ain't a good idea. You'd 'ave a right hard job on your hands then, let me tell you.'

'But Bracken huh, huh, huh … isn't scared … huh, huh . . . of any huh … thing, Dad.'

'That may be so, lass,' said Ned. 'But I think it best if you leave it up to your old dad. I knows a thing or two about beasts, you know.'

'Dad hu, hu … I lie awake dreaming huh, huh … about huh … being able huh, huh, huh … to ride him huh…'

Hearing his daughter's rasping breath and seeing her pursed mouth as she tried to speak, Ned put a finger softly to her lips. 'Hush now, girl. You just lie back in this old comfy chair. Let me do the talking. Now then, there'll be no riding Bracken until you're up, fit and well, so you just concentrate all your energy on getting better and leave Bracken to me. Have we a deal?'

Ned held out his hand. As Jess weakly took hold of it, Christine came into the room carrying a tray with three bowls of steaming broth. 'Enough of your chatter, you two. It's time you got some goodness inside you.'

The three of them ate in Jess's bedroom. Ned cleaned his bowl and Christine, in between feeding Jess, did likewise but Jess could only manage a few spoons of the soup.

Chapter 14
LIFE GOES ON

IN SPITE OF Jess's illness, life went on. Work on the farm could not stop: cows needed milking; hens needed feeding; sheep had to be herded to new pastures. Besides the animals, there was the land. It needed nourishing, ploughing. There were crops to gather, boundary walls and fences to mend. But as he went about his work, Ned thought it all seemed different somehow.

The days seemed longer. He did not smile as much without Jess running round and continually pestering him. Ned kept up a bold appearance, though, and always had a smile when he went up to her bedroom even though smiling was the last thing he felt like doing. The truth was he hated her being unwell and missed the life she brought to the farm and the sound of her laughter about the place. He knew he wasn't the only one that missed her. It seemed like the cows didn't bellow as loudly, the newborn lambs didn't leap so high and Bracken's sparkle and mischief had faded.

Jess had a daily routine before she became ill of going down to the horses' field and giving them both a treat. She shouted their names before clambering up and sitting on the white gate, swinging her legs as she watched Molly and Bracken make their way over. Molly always took her time, her hindquarters swaying slowly from side to side, but Bracken was the complete opposite of his mother. It did not matter where he was in the field, at the far end down at the warren, in the middle or at the top; as soon as he heard Jess call, he raced to her, drawing to a quick stop when he reached the gate and immediately sticking out his big tongue to lick Jess's ear. It was a joy for Ned to see his daughter and the maturing young horse together; now he missed it and longed for the day when Jess would be well again.

Over the following months, the doctor's visits grew fewer as Jess started to show some signs of improvement. She still struggled woefully for breath and was very weak; the simplest of movements was a mammoth task but at least she had stopped coughing blood and the fever and sweats were less frequent.

The doctor had said that it would take a long time for Jess to pull through and he was proved right. More than sixteen months passed before she was out of bed and moving delicately about the house. She was still weak and there was still a grey pallor about her complexion. It was only to be expected but after what seemed an eternity to Ned and Christine, they felt that at last their prayers had been answered.

They had stayed united as they fought her illness and, at long last, appeared to have won the battle. As time went on, Jess got a little stronger and some colour came back to her cheeks. Then Ned and Christine found they had another fight on their hands but, unlike the last one, this was a pleasure.

Jess wanted to see Bracken, to stroke him, give him an apple and whisper in his ear. She had missed him terribly and was constantly plaguing her mum and dad to let her go down to the field. It became a daily battle between parents and child but, as good as it was for Ned and Christine to see their daughter up and about, they were not going to risk a setback to her health. They told Jess repeatedly, 'You will not be allowed out of the house or down to see Bracken until the doctor has examined you and announced you well enough to go outside and play. Now let that be an end to it, Jess.'

For the next few days, Christine repeated, 'Jess, you will remain indoors until such time as the doctor says otherwise and gives his approval. Now let that be an end to the matter.' But it was not. As soon as Ned walked in through the door at night, Jess started pestering him and pleading. Hearing her daughter, Christine appeared as if by magic, framed in the kitchen door at the other end of the narrow limestone hallway. She gave Ned a stern look before he had time to open his mouth and stood watching, arms folded across her breast while Ned answered his daughter. 'No. How many times have I got to tell you, Jess?' Then he looked at Christine and smiled. 'I thinks our daughter's well on mend,' he said and gave her a wink and a nod.

Chapter 15
A STEP OUTSIDE

NED WAS IN the farmyard fixing a wagon. Earlier in the week he had gone into town to the market with a wagonload of sheep he was hoping to sell at auction. He had been late setting off and wanted to get there in good time to register the animals with the auctioneer before the start of the sale and have a look round at the other livestock on offer. As he drove the wagon he knew he was probably going a bit too fast; in his haste, he didn't notice the large pothole in the road. Both the front and back nearside wheels of the wagon crashed down into it. Ned reined in Molly, stopped the wagon and got down to check for damage.

The front wheel appeared to be okay but straight away he noticed the felloes had cracked on the back one, along with a couple of spokes. It was most probably the weight of the animals in the back when he hit the hole that caused the break in the rear wheel. He thought the wheel would hold until he reached the market, offloaded the sheep and hopefully, with the wagon lighter, the damaged wheel would last long enough to get him home in one piece.

He was right; after the sale Ned managed to get himself and the empty wagon safely home without any further mishap. However, he could not risk using the wagon again until he had fixed the wheel. So today Ned was working on the wagon. He was in the process of gradually slipping another block of wood under the axle so the wagon's weight was supported by more than the hydraulic jack when Bracken caught his attention.

The horse was cantering across the field toward the white gate. Ned knew this was a sign that someone was coming up the lane. Sure enough, a black car he recognised as the doctor's Austin turned into the farm. Ned placed another block of timber under the wagon's axle as the doctor drove up and parked in the farmyard. Then he wiped his hands on the bottom of his shirt and went over to greet him.

As he got out of his car, the doctor said, 'Good morning to you, Ned.'

'Morning, doctor.'

'Beautiful day today. Looks like summer's here at long last.'

'Aye, you're right there, doctor. Looks like it may stay like this for a couple of days, I shouldn't wonder.'

'Let's hope so. How's Jess doing?'

'Well, you'll be a lot more qualified than me to answer that question. Come inside and see for yourself.'

Ned opened the front door and shouted, 'Christine, Jess, t'doctor's here.'

The kitchen door opened and Christine appeared, an apron wrapped round her waist, her hands white with flour. 'Hello there, doctor. You'll have to excuse us, me and Jess are just doing some baking. Please come in. I expect you wouldn't mind a nice cup of tea and some fresh-baked biscuits while you're having a look at Jess.'

'That would be rather nice,' replied the doctor as he walked into the kitchen with Ned, remembering to add, 'White, one sugar, please.'

The doctor put his briefcase on the kitchen table. He opened it and pulled out his stethoscope while asking Jess if she would lift up her cardigan and vest. After the examination the doctor packed his equipment and, as Christine poured the tea, adding a splash of milk and one spoonful of sugar, he placed his medical bag on the floor and sat down.

Christine offered the freshly made biscuits. 'I don't mind if I do,' said the doctor helping himself to a digestive. 'It's not often I get offered a biscuit these days, what with the recession and all. People are really starting to feel the pinch, you know. I notice on my rounds everyone appears to be cutting down on life's little luxuries.' Then he enquired, 'How are things with you and the farm, Ned?'

Ned really didn't know where to start. 'Well, I'll tell you like it is, doctor. The farm is just about holding its own at present but when I say "just about", I mean just about. The price at market for the beasts has come down and produce has taken a hefty tumble compared to what I was getting a month or so ago. I can but hope the worst of slump is over but, to be honest, I don't think it is. I had a man round from dairy t'other day and he was telling me to expect a letter from Wilkinson's about a new contract. At times like these it can only mean one thing: they want to reduce the price they are paying for me milk. And if that be the case I'll be struggling, I don't mind telling thee.'

'Now, now Ned,' Christine interrupted. 'We'll not have any negative talk round the table. Besides, the good doctor hasn't come all the way up here to listen to our affairs, he's more important matters to discuss. Isn't that right, doctor?' She changed the topic of the conversation to what concerned her most. 'Tell me, doctor, how is Jess coming on?'

Before answering, the doctor looked towards Jess who sat at the end of the table and gave her a nod and a grin. 'She is doing splendidly. We still have to remember how poorly she was though, and err on the side of caution and take things slowly. At this stage there is nothing to gain by rushing and risking a setback. Slow and steady is the way to win this race.'

'Can I go outside to play?' Jess asked, unable to hold back her desperation to get outside any longer. 'It's so boring having to stay inside all the time. Please, can I? Please?'

Ned was about to scold Jess; the doctor would tell her when she was good and ready and she should hold her tongue and show a little more respect. But he saw the eagerness in her face and before he had a chance to open his mouth, the doctor had started to answer.

'Yes, Jess, I think you are fit enough to venture outdoors now as long as you promise you won't overdo things. No more than an hour or so a day at first, until your lungs get stronger and your breathing is better. You promise me you'll take things easy?'

'I do,' replied Jess, adding quickly, 'It will be so good to get out and see Bracken and Molly. I promise I will stay out no longer than an hour and if I feel tired at any time I'll come straight back in and rest. I promise, I promise.'

'Good for you then,' said the doctor and he could not help but smile at seeing her so excited.

He sipped his tea, helped himself to another biscuit, then looked at his wristwatch and exclaimed, 'My, my, look at the time! I'm afraid I've overstayed my welcome. I have other patients to see today. I must be off.' He swallowed down the last of his tea. 'Don't bother getting up for me, I'll see myself out. You stay where you are and finish those splendid biscuits. Must dash. Thanks once again for the tea.' He hurried from the kitchen, along the limestone hallway and out of the front door.

Bracken, grazing in the field near the white gate, heard the farmhouse door open. He raised his big head and saw the doctor leave the house, go to his car, begin to open the driver's door, hesitate, then go back and knock on the farmhouse door.

The door opened quickly and Jess stood in the doorway, holding out the doctor's leather briefcase. 'Thanks, Jess,' said the

83

doctor. 'I'm sure I'd forget my head at times if it wasn't screwed on.'

As Jess feigned a laugh, a loud nicker resounded from the horse's field. Both Jess and the doctor looked over and saw Bracken, head raised tall, tail swishing. As they watched, he reared, bucked and reared again, neighing even louder.

The doctor, turning back to Jess, smiled. 'I think he's pleased to see you!'

'Isn't he wonderful?' said Jess, looking pleadingly at the doctor. 'I've so missed him. Can I go and see him now, doctor? Right now?'

Glancing at his watch once more, the doctor replied, 'As late as I am for my next appointment, I wouldn't miss this for the world.' He took hold of Jess's hand and together they walked down to the white gate, Bracken bucking and neighing for all he was worth at seeing Jess after all this time.

Chapter 16

TRAINED TO WORK FOR WHAT?

IT WAS TIME for Bracken to start earning his keep.

Watching Bracken's antics as he fearlessly careered round the field, you would never realise a young horse's bones and joints are so soft and fragile. Ned knew, though, and to prevent injury to Bracken, he had not made any heavy demands on the horse other than ensuring the young stallion was halter broken and knew a few basic commands. Bracken was older now; his bones were solid and his joints were strong. It was time he was put to work.

To get Bracken familiar with the horse-drawn machinery around the farm, Ned led Molly and Bracken up to the farmyard where he kept the wagon, tied Bracken to it, then harnessed Molly. He took his time fitting Molly with the collar, bridle, harness, all the while keeping one eye on Bracken and noting how he reacted. With the harness fitted, Ned backed Molly between the shafts and attached the traces and breeching to the wagon. He did all this carefully, ensuring Molly stayed calm and Bracken sensed no fear.

On market days when he was going into town, to familiarise the horse and show him there was nothing to fear, Ned made sure Bracken was there as he lowered the back ramp of the wagon and herded the livestock on board or loaded it with cauliflowers or potatoes.

When Ned felt Bracken was used to the wagon, he started

taking him into town. Turning the wagon round in the yard, Ned set off down the lane, turned right at the bottom and headed for the farmers' market with Bracken, tethered, trotting alongside as Molly pulled the wagon. This introduced Bracken to new sights and sounds and, once again, taught the horse that there was nothing to fear. In this manner both man and animal gained confidence and trust in one another. Ned often wondered, though, why he bothered to adopt this slow approach to training. Bracken was quick to learn and never seemed shy or nervous of anything; Bracken appeared fearless.

It was the same when Ned introduced Bracken to the plough. He brought both horses into the field he was going to work that day, tied Bracken loosely to one of the handles and harnessed up Molly. As he set to ploughing, going up and down the field, Bracken walked alongside. After doing this a few times Bracken, as if to say, 'I understand, I know what's expected of me,' pulled the loose tether free with a flick of his head. He walked off as if he were bored with the proceedings and went to graze, tail swishing gently in an unploughed part of the meadow.

During this time, Jess didn't get to see Bracken as much as she would have liked. She was mindful of the promise she had made to the doctor about taking things easy and not staying out for more than an hour or so a day. Truth be told, even if she had wanted to, she was not able. She still laboured with her breathing and at the end of each day she was exhausted. Tiredness did not stop her plaguing Ned when he walked through the door at night, however. The first words her father heard as he entered the kitchen and went to wash his hands were, 'How did Bracken do today, Dad? Tell me everything.' The whole family listened as, between each mouthful of food, Ned recounted the day's events.

'Damn horse acts as if he knows everything, so he does. I swear he looks at me as if I'm some kind of idiot. It's me that's teaching him but you'd think it was t'other way round. I went to plough t'corner field today and took both horses. After a few minutes ploughing, Bracken flicks that big head of his, pulls his tether free and walks off, grand as you like. Finds himself a nice quiet part of the field he does, and starts to nibble the grass as calm as can be. I thought, oh well, might as well leave him, no use forcing the animal. So I carries on ploughing but after a while I gets an itch on my back, right between my shoulder blades. I tries scratching it and I've just got me fingers to where it's right itchy, and I'm a bit distracted what with one arm on t'plough and t'other over my shoulder, so I goes a bit off t'straight with the furrow. But when I finish scratching and sees what I've done I also notice Bracken. He's there, looking me full on and he shakes that big head of his slowly from side to side as if to say, "Dearie me, you've made a bit of a mess there, haven't you?" Laughing at me, he were. Anyway, I'll tell you what, training tomorrow has finished for him. From now on he won't be watching Molly any more, Molly can watch him for a change. Tomorrow I'm goin' to finish off ploughing the field and it will be Bracken pulling t'plough this time. We'll see how good he is then, won't we? Mr Know-it-all Horse – in all me years of farming I've never seen the like of such a beast.'

Ned was so serious that by the time their plates were finished Jess was sore with laughing; Christine laughed, too!

Having Bracken as a distraction was a blessing in this time of poverty and struggle. At least the Bradshaws had something to laugh about; many had not. Over the year the recession continued to bite and bite hard. The price of livestock tumbled and crops were now selling at less than sixty per cent of cost. Ned was seriously worried about the financial state of the farm. He had not mentioned anything to Christine but she knew something was troubling him and, aware of the times they were living in, knew only too well what that something might be.

On her trips into town she saw charity soup kitchens along the streets, with queues of people standing miserably in line waiting to get a free handout of a bowl of gruel and, if they were lucky, a piece of dried bread. All you heard on people's lips these days was talk of the recession. The newspapers were full of it. Headlines stated that millions were now unemployed and the newsreaders on the wireless reported almost hourly on how the recession was gripping the country. Christine had heard one reporter say only the other day that in some areas unemployment was as high as seventy per cent. She hoped the government's National Unemployment and Health Insurance Scheme* would help those unfortunates but she knew it only paid out for a maximum of fifteen weeks. The millions of long-term unemployed and their families were left without any source of income at all. What happened to them she shuddered to think.

After all their talk, what are the politicians doing, Christine asked herself. When the war was won they pledged to make Britain a place fit for heroes. They said it for all to hear. Every house with a wireless set, anyone who could read a newspaper, was witness to their pledge. Surely they would not allow the people to suffer in peacetime? Surely those on high, the aristocrats, the gentry, lords and ladies and others in high office had seen enough suffering? Had The Great War taught them nothing?

Had the lords and ladies forgotten how the common man had fought? How they suffered and died. Surely they would reward the people by coming to their aid? Surely they knew to create a better world through kindness, decency and humanity? They had the influence and power; surely they would do something to help the likes of those poor hungry souls waiting wretchedly outside the soup kitchens! There again, perhaps they were too greedy, too self-centred and would not.

Christine knew they were fortunate to be living on the farm. Nevertheless, her thoughts were gloomy as she recalled Ned's behaviour and the letter he'd recently received. The envelope

---

* Introduced in 1911

had Wilkinson Dairy Ltd stamped in red ink in the top left-hand corner.

Seeing the dairy stamp and fearing the worst, Christine had filled the kettle, waited for it to boil, held the spout up to the envelope and steamed it open. Wilkinson's wrote saying they were losing money and could no longer buy milk at the present price. If Ned wanted to continue selling to them, it must be at the new lower rate as set out in the letter. As Christine saw the miserable price they were offering her stomach curdled.

If Ned accepted, he would be selling at a loss. But what option did he have; who else would buy their milk? She refolded the letter and put it back inside the envelope, laying it flat on the kitchen table. Pressing down hard, she ran her palm along the gummed edge and resealed it. Ned would never know she had opened it and she would not mention it to him. He had enough on his mind, what with Jess's illness and all the hours he spent running the farm. She didn't want him to worry about her as well. No, the best thing she could do was to keep quiet, pretend everything was fine and keep a cheerful countenance. So she laughed with her daughter when Ned came in off the farm and told his tales of Bracken but all the time, beneath her smile, she was troubled, deeply troubled, about what lay ahead for them all.

Chapter 17
RIGHT WORK, RIGHT REWARD

NED'S HEAD WAS full of money worries; he had another restless night.

Christine lay beside him feigning sleep as he tossed and turned. Ned would talk to her in his own time; until then she would keep her counsel.

Ned woke with dark bags under his eyes. He pulled on his breeches and fastened his shirt as he went downstairs to the kitchen. With his breakfast barely touched, he got up from the table and, after fastening his boots by the door, went outside and walked down to the white gate. He called Bracken over. Today he would take the horse up to the meadow and Bracken would earn his keep. Today Bracken would pull the blades that churned the soil and Molly would have a day off.

Bracken stood strong in front of the plough.

Ned fitted the collar and harness to the horse, noting Bracken's calmness, but he was puzzled when he tightened the last straps to feel a slight tremor run across the horse's flanks. His mind was full of worries and he had a field to work, so didn't dwell on it as he took up his position between the handles of the plough.

'Today we'll see just how good you are, Mister Smarty-pants Horse. Move on,' he called and flicked the reins. Bracken took up the strain, the blades bit into the ground and the soil began to turn.

Bracken moved at a steady pace, laying down one straight furrow after another as he effortlessly pulled the plough up and down the field.

An hour or more passed, enough time for Bracken to become used to the plough. Then Ned felt Bracken pick up speed. 'Whoa there,' said Ned. 'You're doing just fine now. No need to tire yourself out. Slow down.'

Bracken was not for listening; his pace increased further. Ned quickened his stride to keep up.

'Whoa, boy! I said whoa!' cried Ned. But the more he shouted, the faster Bracken went. 'For crikey's sake slow down.' The horse was not for listening. Ned could see Bracken's mighty muscles bulging as he strained, the plough churning up the clay soil at greater speed. 'Slow down boy, slow down!' shouted Ned. 'For mercy's sake slow down.'

Almost running, Ned reined Bracken in, hauling back on the reins as hard as he could – but to no avail. The horse powered on.

Ned fought the reins and dug his feet into the earth with no effect. Then all of a sudden he recalled the tremor he'd seen running through Bracken's flanks, the same tremor he heard athletes experienced before the beginning of a big race and the firing of the starter's gun. He understood now: Bracken was testing himself. Treating this like a game. The horse wanted to see how well it could plough and, having found it easy, wanted to make the game harder and more challenging. Bracken was turning it into a race, a race to see how quickly he could plough the entire meadow.

Ned joined in the game; after all the stress he had been under, he embraced it! 'Yee ha, come on boy, I'm with you!' he shouted, encouraging the horse. 'Go on, boy! Go on, go on!' he yelled, holding on to the plough and running even faster to keep up and not hamper Bracken's efforts. 'Come on, let's go.' Ned was enraptured, his worries forgotten, completely caught up in the game.

Man and animal raced up and down the meadow. Up and down they went, time after time, Bracken using his might, blowing, snorting, heaving as straight line after straight line formed in the wake of the churning plough. Behind him, Ned hollered encouragement and laughed like an excited schoolboy, feeling alive as man and animal worked in harmony and raced to plough the field as fast as they possibly could.

With the sun low in the sky and casting its red glow, stallion and man stood at the top of the field, job done. Bracken was lathered in sweat. Ned breathed heavily, elated; mere words could not express how he felt.

Exhilarated, tired, his shirt soaked in perspiration, Ned softly caressed Bracken's muzzle. Bracken stood, strong, noble, with the heart of a lion, enjoying Ned's gentle touch. All Ned's doubts were well and truly vanquished as he saw the full magnificence of the horse before him.

As he softly stroked the horse, Ned's feeling of euphoria fell away. He moved his head forward and rested it on Bracken's withers; with one arm over the stallion's back, feeling the horse's might against him, he began to sob. The tears ran freely down his face; he couldn't have stopped them if he'd tried. The strain of seeing Jess so poorly these many months, the sleepless nights he and Christine had endured as they nursed her, the long hours of hard work on the farm, the financial difficulties – it had all been too much. The game he and Bracken had just played had released the stress he had long endured. As his tears fell over Bracken's brown coat, the strain fell from his shoulders and his mood lifted once more. Finally, as the sun sank behind the hills and cast its last fingers of light across the vale, man and animal headed home.

Ned took his time rubbing Bracken down in the barn before

walking him back to the field. As Bracken sauntered over to Molly, Ned went to the old bathtub, took off his shirt and scooped water up over his chest and face. He paid particular attention to his eyes; no point in letting the womenfolk know he'd been crying. As he dried himself on his shirt, he made up his mind: when he got Christine alone he would tell her about the dire situation they were in. He knew he could no longer carry the burden alone.

Chapter 18
A TALE OF BRACKEN

NED TOOK OFF his boots in the hallway and walked through to the kitchen in his stockinged feet. Christine, her pinny wrapped round her, was at the stove stirring a pot of boiling vegetables. Jess was slumped on the table; he noticed she looked tired and a bit off colour but as Ned came through the door she sprang up and started bombarding him with questions, wanting to know what Bracken had been up to. No matter her pale complexion, Ned thought; the colour would soon come flooding back to her cheeks once she heard his latest tale.

'How did the ploughing go, Dad? Was he any good? Please tell, please,' Jess implored.

'First things first, lass,' said Ned going over to the sink. He washed his hands under the tap. 'Once we're all sat down and your mother's got t'meal on t'table I'll tell you. Your mother will want to hear as well and you know just as good as I do that she can't do two things at once, like cook and listen.'

'You cheeky thing,' said Christine, picking up the wet dishcloth by the sink and playfully throwing it at him. Jess laughed as Ned caught the wet rag in his soapy hands and threw it back at his wife.

'Enough, enough!' retorted Christine. 'The cloth nearly landed in the soup. You just hurry on and get your hands dried, Ned Bradshaw, and less of your nonsense. I'm about to serve up.'

As they ate Ned told them about Bracken ploughing the field. 'He were amazing. He started off at a steady enough pace, each furrow as straight as could be. I was thinking he were not bad, in fact if I'm honest, I was thinking he were pretty darn good. Anyway, after ploughing a few furrows I was just beginning to settle in to a steady day's work when all of a sudden...' Ned picked up some bread and tore off a chunk, stuck it in his mouth, followed by a spoonful of soup.

'All of a sudden what, Dad? Stop eating and tell us!' shouted Jess impatiently, all excited.

Ned, knowing how she would react, slowly and deliberately chewed his food. 'Rude to talk with your mouth full,' he said, talking with his mouth full. Then he broke off another chunk of bread and slipped it into his mouth, teasing Jess and drawing out the drama.

'Dad,' said Jess, 'you're doing this on purpose. You're so mean. Tell us! What did Bracken do? We want to know, don't we, Mum?'

Christine looked up from her soup and raised her eyebrows. 'Ned, you are awful. Stop teasing the girl and tell her.'

Ned resumed. 'As I was saying, Bracken was ploughing furrows as straight as I'd ever seen and I'm starting to relax, seeing what a good job he's doing, when all of a sudden he starts to quicken his pace. I shouts to him to slow down but the more I shouts the quicker he tries to go. I haul back on the reins to make him go slower but it's no use, t'horse is so powerful. He goes faster. I'm shouting at him, pulling back on t'reins with all me might but nothing is working; he's going faster. Nothing I do is stopping him. He's deliberately ignoring me, trying to go even faster.' Ned stopped talking, took hold of a mug of tea and drank a mouthful.

'Dad,' whined Jess.

'Okay, okay,' said Ned. 'It's thirsty work, all this talking.'

Christine raised her eyebrows again and looked at him.

'I'm getting desperate by now,' continued Ned, resuming the

story. 'How the dickens am I going to get this horse under control? And then, all of a sudden, I have an inspiration.' Again Ned paused and took up another spoon of soup, his action met by the same response: raised eyebrows from Christine, a moan from Jess. Ned carried on. 'I had this inspiration, see. It dawned on me what Bracken was doing. He was playing a game to see how well and how quick he could finish ploughing t'field. Once I understood, I picked my feet up, gave him free rein and cheered him on. You should have seen him go, he was magnificent. We must have looked a right sight for sore eyes, the two of us. If anyone had seen us they would have thought we were running in front of the King at Royal Ascot rather than ploughing up an old carrot field.'

Ned drank some more soup. 'You won't believe me but you can go up and see for yourselves. We ploughed whole meadow, we did!'

'Never,' exclaimed Christine. 'Stop joking us, Ned. That meadow has never taken less than two full days to plough.'

'I'm telling you, Christine, ploughing over in yon meadow is finished and each and every furrow is as straight as straight can be.'

'You're not funning us, Dad, are you?'

'No, Jess, you can both go up and see for yourselves tomorrow morning. In all me years of farming I've never come across an animal quite like that Bracken. He's a good 'un he is, something really special.'

'I told you he was,' said Jess. 'Didn't I tell you he was?' With that, the conversation stopped as they finished their meal, the food filling their bellies and thoughts of Bracken filling their heads.

When everyone finished eating, Christine filled the kettle and set it on the stove to boil. Ned and Jess cleared the table. With the bowls, plates, knives and spoons in the sink, Jess asked, 'Mum, is it alright if I don't do the dishes tonight? I feel a bit tired and I think I'll go up to my bedroom for a lie down.'

Before Christine had a chance to reply, Ned spoke up. 'Not a problem, my sweet. You go on up and I'll dry the pots.'

Jess left the kitchen and Ned and Christine heard her footsteps slowly pad up the wooden stairs and across the landing to her room.

The water boiled. Christine lifted the kettle and poured the hot water over the dishes. She was concerned. She had made a pact with herself that she would not mention any of her worries to Ned; he had enough on his mind. However, there were priorities; money worries were one thing but the health of her daughter was quite another.

As the two of them stood with the steam of the hot water rising from the sink, Christine asked Ned, 'Have you noticed how tired Jess has looked over the last couple of days? You don't think her sickness is coming back, do you, Ned? It can't, can it, not after all this time and her doing so well?'

Ned paused and took a deep breath before replying. Christine's question had caught him completely off guard. He had noticed Jess's pallor and tiredness as soon as he walked into the kitchen but Jess had looked tired, not sick. Having come through such a severe illness there were bound to be times when she looked a bit drained. After all, the doctor had said her recovery would be slow. He took another deep breath, throwing the tea towel over his shoulder as he pondered.

He hadn't noticed anything untoward about his daughter's health. Could it be he hadn't noticed anything wrong because his mind was full of the recession and the financial state of the farm? Had he been too preoccupied with his own problems to see a change for the worse in Jess? Or was Christine just being a mother and, like most mothers, being over-protective of her child? He was not sure; either way, he considered Jess did not look too bad. She had joined in having a bit of a carry-on at the table with the story of Bracken's ploughing and he felt that was a good sign.

Having thought the matter through, Ned spoke. 'She's most probably done a little too much today, that's all, love. I think you're just being a bit anxious and worrying unduly. Let's see how she is tomorrow, after a good night's sleep.'

Christine was glad she had Ned by her side. With all his worries, she thought, he can still find time to come up with the right words to comfort me. Smiling softly, she said, 'You're most probably right, Ned Bradshaw. Now get that towel off your shoulder and start drying these dishes.'

However, as they washed and put away the pots and pans, their thoughts were no longer on Bracken and the ploughed field but focused firmly on their daughter's health.

Chapter 19
TROUBLES SHARED

IT SEEMED ALL Jess needed was a good night's sleep after all as next day, and over the coming weeks, her condition continued to improve. The state of the farm did not, however.

Ned continued to work as hard – harder, if that were possible – round the place. He cut back to the bone on expenditure, spending only on the barest of essentials. Yet with the prices he was getting at the markets and the lower price he was forced to accept from Wilkinson's for the milk, there simply was not enough money to pay the bills and cover the outgoings. To make up the shortfall, Ned had been dipping into their savings over the preceding months. He tried hard, so very hard, to be as frugal as possible with their money. It had taken them many years to build up their meagre nest egg but now, in only a few months, their savings were all gone.

Ned had only one option. He saddled up Bracken before going into the farmhouse and up the stairs to his and Christine's bedroom. He went to the double wardrobe and removed his Sunday-best black suit, white shirt and black tie and laid them on the bed. He took his bowler hat from the top of the wardrobe and tossed it alongside his clothes. Stripping off his work clothes, he started to get changed.

Down in the kitchen, Christine was baking bread. She thought she heard someone come into the house and a minute later was sure when she heard Ned's footsteps going up the stairs. That's odd, she thought, Ned doesn't usually come in at this time of day. I wonder if anything's the matter?

She rubbed her hands on her red-and-white striped pinny and went up the stairs. Ned was tying his shoelaces. 'Is everything all right?' she quizzed.

Ned looked up, frowning. He had wanted to confide in her before but he had never found the opportunity. He thought this was as good a time as any. 'No, love, everything's not all right. It hasn't been all right for a long time now. I have something to tell you.'

Christine sat down beside Ned and took hold of his hand, gently pulling it onto her lap as he continued. 'I've tried to keep things from you, what with Jess been poorly and all. You've had enough to cope with. But knowing you as I do, I think you can already guess what I'm about to tell you.'

Christine looked into her husband's eyes and slowly nodded her head. 'I think I can, Ned. I think I can. How bad is it?'

'Very bad, love. This recession we're in, nobody is buying anything. Every time I go down to the market I'm coming back with nearly as many vegetables as I go down with. Livestock isn't selling either; no one can afford to buy meat. And the dairy – after all these years of me dealing with them, I've had to drop the price of the milk otherwise they said they wouldn't buy it. I had no choice and the buggers knew it. Now we're making nowt on the milk either.'

'I know,' Christine said softly. 'I know.'

'I've been using our savings to try and keep the farm afloat, hoping that we could see ourselves through until this dammed slump comes to an end but there's no sign of that happening, is there?' Ned dropped his head, saying quietly under his breath, 'Damn those buggers who caused this. Damn them all.'

He turned to Christine. 'I've got an appointment with the bank manager, love. I'm hoping he will lend us some money. I'd best go otherwise I'll be late.' He swept up his bowler hat, kissed Christine on the forehead and went down the stairs and out of the front door.

Christine remained on the bed for a while after Ned had gone. She was surprised by the mixture of emotions she was feeling. She knew she should be worried. Things must be bad for Ned to have talked so openly and now all their savings were gone. But strangely, rather than being afraid of what the future held for her and her family, she felt a sense of relief.

The truth was out; Ned had finally opened up to her. Knowing him as she did, she knew that he would feel better for doing so. He had tried to hide matters to protect them, kept things to himself and put on a brave face for her and Jess's sake. She had seen how he struggled to fall asleep, restlessly tossing and turning when he did, his subconscious wrestling with problems, searching for answers. If he carried on bottling things up inside, she had no doubt it would make him ill – and she'd been through enough illness with Jess.

She remembered the night the doctor arrived and told them Jess had consumption, the fear she had felt in the pit of her stomach, the utter despair at the thought that she might lose her child to that dreaded disease. She did not want to go through the same thing with Ned. Far better, she thought, that they all had their health. As long as all three of them were together, that was the main thing; nothing mattered to her more than Ned and Jess.

She felt relief at having sorted out the correct order of priorities. Yes, she thought, as long as they were all together things would work out. Nevertheless, as she rose from the bed her thoughts were on more practical matters.

She had seen the dishevelled lines of sinewy people queuing up outside the soup kitchens; the thought of her family having to stand in line brought her out in goosebumps and made her shiver. She hoped that Ned would be successful in getting a loan from the bank. The money would tide them over to the end of this awful slump. They would be all right then, wouldn't they? Surely this awful recession could not go on for much longer. The downturn had to end soon.

Chapter 20
BOYS WILL BE BOYS

NED, BOWLER PERCHED securely on top of his head, sat proudly on Bracken; the horse had that effect on you and made you feel special, even though Ned knew he had no right to feel special, especially today. Call it by any other name, today he was going cap in hand to beg the bank manager for a loan. However, dressed in his finery with Bracken beneath him and the horse's golden-brown coat gleaming with health, Ned looked swell and dandy and anything but a beggar as he rode along the road.

Halfway into town Ned spied two boys walking alongside the road ahead. He recognised them as Billy Robertson and his partner in crime, Ralph Slinn. They were passing something between them but, at this distance, Ned could not make out what it was.

Billy and Ralph, two urchins well known in the area, had a reputation for being a couple of right scallywags. Ned had encountered them before and had first-hand experience of their escapades. He had caught them red-handed on the farm several times, trying to steal eggs from his chicken coop. Each time he had given them a clip round the ear and a severe telling off before letting them go with a tap on the backside from his size nine-and-a-half boot for good measure. He had his suspicions they were responsible for more than just a few eggs going missing: a hen or two had also mysteriously disappeared. Maybe he should have been firmer and given them a really good scare by reporting them to the police and letting the constabulary deal with them; a scolding and a kick up the rear from him had not seemed to dent their interest in his eggs.

In spite of this, Ned was of the opinion that boys will be boys; besides, he knew that both these lads had not had the best starts in life and had it tough at home. They were both fatherless, their dads having been killed in The Great War like so many others. God knows how their mothers coped without a husband in this slump. They would most probably be glad when the boys were a bit older so they could get jobs down the pits. That is, if the coal mines ever opened again.

Ned had heard recently that many of the mines had shut down, the gates padlocked. In some areas unemployment was as high as twenty-five per cent amongst the miners. He felt sorry for the unemployed, really sorry. There again, he knew about the conditions down the pits, especially for the children. Thank the Lord for the 1900 Prohibition Act preventing children under the age of thirteen years working down them. Perhaps it would be better if the collieries never opened again.

But that was an issue to think about another day. Today he had to concentrate on dealing with the bank manager and getting that loan instead of wondering what these two young rascals were up to.

As Ned reflected, Bracken drew level with the two boys.

'Afternoon, Mr Ned,' Billy said cockily, tipping his flat cap.

'You off to a funeral, are ya?' voiced Ralph, scratching his armpit and seeing Ned in a black suit, white shirt with a black bowler perched on his head.

Ralph had only been to one funeral, his dad's. He stood at the graveside, fascinated, and watched the coffin being lowered by the pallbearers into the freshly dug grave. When he looked up, he found he was hemmed in on all sides by grown-ups, men and women all dressed in black. The women wore veils over their faces and looked creepy; the men wore big black hats and looked extra tall. They all looked threatening to young Ralph and he did not like it. He felt the mourners crowding in on him, pushing him forward, pushing him into the grave. His skin became clammy, his breathing shallow and he fainted. He was so traumatised by the event that from that day forth seeing anyone dressed in black triggered memories of the burial of his father's empty coffin*.

On the day of his father's funeral, the coffin was empty because his body was never returned home after the war. Nevertheless they scraped together what money they could as it was only proper and decent to hold a funeral service out of respect for a brave man. Other families did the same; many, not having sufficient money and unable to cover the expense, only wished that they could.

'No, Ralph. Just because I've got my finery on doesn't mean I'm going to a funeral,' replied Ned. 'Less about my business, by the way, and more about yours. For a start, what's that thing you're holding?' Ned now addressed Billy, not quite believing what he saw in the boy's hands; it was a miniature steel crossbow. The barrel of the weapon measured about eight inches and appeared to have a small wind-up mechanism for tensioning the bow. The bow itself was about the same length as the barrel. 'What in heaven's name

---

* The Battle of the Somme started on the 1st July 1916. By the end of the battle, the British had lost 420,000 troops. The battle was orchestrated by Field Marshal Douglas Haig, 1st Earl of Bermersyde. Lord Kitchener, a politician, holding the position Secretary of State for War at that time, endorsed the battle plans. Both Earl and Lord were keen supporters of the theory of attrition – grind your enemy down and eventually they would have to yield. Haig gave the order time after time, after bloody time for his troops to leave what little safety the trenches offered and 'go over the top'. The men obeyed, carrying out their orders, believing that their aristocratic Field Marshal knew best. Haig knowingly sacrificed over 400,000 men to gain, and then lose again, a few yards of land. Both Billy and Ralph's fathers were reported as fatally wounded during the battle but later found seriously injured, survived and went on to serve king and country until nearing the end of the war when they were both killed in minor skirmishes.

are you doing with that thing?' exclaimed Ned. 'And where did you get it?'

'It were me dad's,' said Billy, running his hands along the weapon. 'Got it from out of his box of things that t'soldier delivered to t'house after t'war, didn't I? All that were left of 'im were in that box. Me dad were a reet good shot with this. He could hit a rabbit at a hundred yards, he could. Me mum told me, in't that reet, Ralph?'

Ralph nodded as he carried on scratching his armpit. Billy continued, 'My dad never missed, he didn't. Me mum said. Took it with him when he joined t'army. Said that if he were out in t'middle of no man's land on night patrols, secret like, a rifle was too noisy, it'd give him away. Said he'd use this instead, silent like. T'Huns would never know he were there.'

'And just what do you think you're going to do with that thing now, Billy?'

'Goin' huntin', Mr Ned. Mum's had no proper food in for weeks and I'm t'man about house with me having no dad. It's up to me to catch something for us dinners, like me dad did.'

Ned knew only too well that these were hard times for folk. If Billy and Ralph were lucky enough to catch a rabbit or bring down a bird or two, fair play to them. Food of any kind, especially food that you did not have to pay for, would be very welcome in any household let alone ones like Billy's and Ralph's. With little or no state welfare aid, families were at their wits' end trying to bring their children up on hardly anything at all. Ned was at a loss to know how widows coped and there were many single-parent families; the war had seen to that.

Ned could see that the little crossbow was a lethal weapon. Still, he could not help but think the two rascals would be okay. He assumed they would only use fallen twigs for arrows; they would be lucky if they managed to make anything fly straight, let alone hit something. Ned knew he could not afford to be late for the meeting with the bank manager, so he pushed Bracken on and left the boys to their mischief.

As Bracken and Ned continued on their way, Billy and Ralph turned off the road and headed across the fields making for the nearby woods on the Peculiar Man's estate. As they ran, their long grey socks around their ankles, the six deadly bolts that slotted into the crossbow bounced and jiggled in the back pocket of Billy's grey shorts.

Ned, had he seen these pointed tips of machined and brightly polished steel, might have been more worried over the boys' safety; the fact was, he had not.

Chapter 21
DON'T BANK ON HELP

CHRISTINE WAS ON tenterhooks by the time Ned arrived back from the bank. She rushed into the hallway as she heard him come through the door and searched his face for any sign of whether he had been successful or not in getting the money. He looked sullen and Christine's heart sank as fleeting images of the three of them standing outside a soup kitchen assailed her. She went to wrap her arms round him and comfort him but, as she approached, Ned did not have the heart to keep up his pretence. His face lit up in a big smile. 'We got the loan. The bank gave us t'money.'

On hearing Ned's words, Christine's legs nearly buckled. Joyfully she flung her arms round his neck, hugging and kissing him. They had managed to secure the money from the bank! Ned kissed her back and, as they embraced, the tension they had both felt throughout the day drained away.

Having found comfort in each other, Ned gently took hold of Christine's hands and removed them from his neck. Holding her at arm's length so he could see her face, he said, 'The news isn't as good as you think. I have more to tell you. The bank gave me a loan but not for all the money, see. They gave me a quarter of what I think we'll need. The bank manager said it were enough to see us through to the end of the year. But by my reckonin' it'll barely cover us, if that.'

'But at the end of the year surely you can go back and see if they will let us have some more money? We've been good customers,' said Christine.

'I wouldn't count on it, love. The manager said to think myself lucky. It's only because we're a farm and he's giving us priority. Says he's under strict instructions from head office that loans, private or personal, are not to be issued in these uncertain times. How are the banks to make money if they lend to failing businesses? he asked me. It's only because t'banks recognise that food is still needed and farming is still worth investing in that he is allowed to give us any money at all, is what he said. He also said he sincerely hopes I won't be coming to his door again asking for another loan. He assured me in no uncertain terms that I'd be wasting my time and he would send me away with a flea in my ear if I did!'

'How could he talk to you like that, Ned? We've scrimped and saved all these years just to put a little money aside for when we're old. Okay, so we've used up all our savings now but we needed to in order to get by. That's one of the reasons for having savings, isn't it, to have money that you can call on in an emergency? The bank has used our money all these years and made even more money out of it, for which we hardly see a penny. Most of it goes on paying those fancy bankers their extortionate salaries. The banks toadied up to us when they wanted our business and begged us to open an account with them. Now, when we need them to help us, they turn their backs and treat us shamefully. The way they behave is sickening, it cannot be right,' said Christine, annoyed.

'Calm down, love. What can we do about it? How do you think I felt, having to sit there and listen to him speak to me like that? He made me feel like I was back at school, a naughty child back in the headmaster's office. But I had to sit there and keep me mouth shut and take it, cos if I had said anything, he may not have given us t'money. Anyway, I've had enough for one day, love, and I don't want to talk about it any more. For the moment let's be thankful we have some money and leave it at that.'

'All right then, Ned, but it is so unfair. It really does make my blood boil. Something should be done about those banks,' Christine replied, shaking her head in anger.

'Amen to that, like,' said Ned. 'Now then, girl, how's about a nice cuppa for your husband? I'm fair parched.'

The two of them walked into the kitchen and Christine filled the kettle.

Even though the bank had loaned them only a small portion of the money they needed to keep their heads above water, both Ned and Christine went to bed feeling a little easier that night for having secured the loan. Instead of tossing and turning, Ned went straight to sleep as soon as his head touched the pillow and Christine, feeling her husband more relaxed and not disturbed by his restlessness, was asleep soon after.

A few hours later, they were woken by a loud knocking on the farmhouse door.

Chapter 22
OH DEER, WE'RE HUNGRY

THE MOON CAME out from behind a cloud and silhouetted the two horses, Molly and Bracken, as they lay asleep in the field. Both horses' chests rose and fell as their large lungs filled and exhaled the night air in an easy, restful rhythm. Then there was another movement, not one easily discernible in the sporadic moonlight, and Bracken's nostrils twitched. An unaccustomed smell drifted on the wind: it was the smell of blood. The odour tainted the air, arousing Molly and Bracken. Suddenly there was a dull thump close to where they lay.

Primordial instincts of fright and flight took over and both horses were immediately up on their feet. Molly bolted, taking off across the field, but against all natural instinct Bracken turned and faced the direction from which the sound stemmed. He stood fixed and solid, muscles tensed, ears pricked, alert, straining to detect further menace. All he heard was the exhausted breathing and tremors of a very young and scared animal.

Earlier that evening in the woods on the Peculiar Man's estate, under the cover of twilight, a fallow deer and her fawn came across a fallen ash tree. The trunk was covered with sphagnum moss, a favourite food of the deer. The two animals began to nibble, unaware of the boys concealed down wind only yards away.

The crossbow was primed. Billy turned to Ralph and whispered,

'Shush,' as he put his hand behind his back and removed one of the steel bolts from his pocket. He laid the bolt along the barrel, took aim and fired. The string twanged as the tension came off the bow; the bolt flew along the barrel, through the air and pierced the fawn in the neck.

The boys both saw the bolt enter the young deer. Excited, they jumped up and charged out of their hiding place, scampering over the undergrowth in their haste to capture the small wounded creature.

Panicked by the boys, the deer fled through the woods. The fawn kept up with her mother, following her closely, but soon she began to tire and fall behind and was isolated from her doe.

Billy and Ralph ran after the fawn, crashing and whooping through the trees as they gave chase. Their noise made it easy at first for the young deer to lose them and let her stop every now and then to rest and recover her strength. At rest, her mottled chestnut-and-white speckled coat provided perfect camouflage in the hazy grey-blue twilight of the woods. But as good as her camouflage was, the boys' youthful eyes spotted her and the chase resumed. The fawn sprang forward again, the boys close on her tail.

The boys pursued the young creature well into the night but with every passing minute, the young deer grew weaker. Loss of blood and the tiring struggle to avoid capture were taking their toll.

Gaining a moment's rest, some wild instinct took hold of her; this would be her last chance to evade the boys. She set off once more, a force of nature compelling her to ignore the pain in her aching muscles, driving her on to put distance between herself and the boys. The fawn ran like a will o' the wisp, darting between the trees and over the land, leaving Billy and Ralph far behind.

After an hour of searching fruitlessly, Billy and Ralph finally got bored and gave up looking for the fawn. They made their way through the woods and across the Peculiar Man's estate back to the road, happy that they had had a great adventure. Both of them thought it was a pity they had not caught the fawn but at least they had managed to bag a rabbit and a couple of pigeons. Proud as punch and feeling like the big-game hunters in Africa that they read about in their comics, they walked back home with dirty faces, shirt-tails hanging out, socks around their ankles and boots covered in mud. Their mums would be pleased when they saw the free food they had brought back and neither boy thought he would get a telling-off for coming home dirty and late.

Frantically the fawn ran through the woods until she darted out onto open farmland. She raced across a ploughed field then over another full of leafy cauliflowers; she ran until she was completely exhausted. In one final effort, before her aching legs gave out, she leapt over a hedgerow. She landed, her strength drained, her belly thumping onto the ground. Unable to move, the spent fawn lay trembling, gulping for breath in the horses' field.

A small gap appeared in the cloud allowing moonlight to cast its light upon the land. Bracken stood solid, ears pricked, as the glimmer of moonlight illuminated the slumped outline of the stricken fawn. He moved forward carefully, softly padding as he did when he was young and sneaked up on the timid wild rabbits he used to chase. He nudged the deer gently with his nose. The smell of blood was pungent. He sensed the deer's terror and ran the side of his big head gently along her flanks. It seemed to ease her.

Suddenly Bracken turned from the fawn and galloped off up the field. He passed the nervous Molly who, by her stance, appeared to be alert and ready to take flight again in an instant. Bracken made for the white gate and, in one bound, jumped over and continued his charge up to the farmhouse.

Some basic instinct made Bracken aware that the fawn needed help, help that only Ned, Christine or Jess could give. He stopped outside the front door of the farmhouse and paced several times around the yard. He had watched the two-legged creatures, seen the postman and the doctor take hold of something on the door. It made a sound and the sound brought Ned, Christine or Jess.

Bracken approached the farmhouse door and put his nose to the brass knocker. He raised it slightly before it slipped and landed back on the striker plate with a gentle tap. He stood back and waited for the door to open but nothing happened. He tried again, the knocker once more slipping from his nose with only a quiet rap. No one came to the door. He tried again and failed, and again. He could not lift the knocker high enough for it to make a loud noise.

Bracken was not about to be beaten. He moved away from the door and stood silently. His head nodded slowly for a second before he stepped forward again to the door. He raised his head and looked at the brass knocker but this time he did not stretch out his neck; this time he did not try to lift it with his nose. He lowered his head, raised his right forelock and kicked the door four times with his shoed hoof.

The sound reverberated through the house. 'Ned, Ned, there's someone at the door. Who can it be at this time of night? Get out of bed quickly! Go and see, go and see!' said Christine sitting up in bed, shocked at being woken by the loud banging on the door.

'I hear it, woman. I hear it! I'm going, give me a chance to get me trousers on, for God's sake,' Ned replied drowsily, annoyed at being woken at this time of night. He sat up in bed and threw back the covers.

'Who on earth can it be at this time?'

'I don't know, do I?' said Ned, even more irritably as he pulled up his pants. 'How am I supposed to know until I go down the stairs and open the door?'

Not bothering to put on his socks or shirt, Ned left the bedroom, still fastening up his trousers.

By the time he reached the front door, Christine was halfway down the stairs behind him in her white nightshirt. The loud knocking had also woken Jess and she was out of bed, wrapped in her blue dressing gown, coming down the stairs behind her mother.

As Ned opened the door, a look of surprise spread across his face as he saw Bracken in front of him but no one else. He looked round the door, left then right. Nobody was there.

'Who is it?' asked Christine, reaching the bottom of the stairs.

Bewilderment replaced surprise on Ned's face as he looked outside again before turning round to Christine and Jess. 'There's no one here. Well, no one I can see.'

'What do you mean, no one you can see?' answered Christine, puzzled. 'There has to be someone there. They were knocking loud enough to wake the dead.'

'I tell you, love, there ain't no one here.'

By this time, Jess had nudged past her parents and was peering through the open door. 'Dad,' she said, 'Bracken is here. Don't you think he's acting rather strange? I'm not sure, Dad, and you might think me daft – but do you think he's trying to tell us something?'

All three of them looked at the horse in the yard. Bracken took a few steps toward the white gate before coming back to the farmhouse door, turned and strode off in the direction of the gate. Ned, Christine and Jess watched him. All three of them caught on to what the horse was trying to tell them. It was Jess, though, who said what they were all thinking. 'I think he wants us to follow him. Bracken wants us to go with him!'

Ned was already gathering his boots and putting them on. 'You stay here and I'll see what he wants.'

'No,' said Jess. 'I'm coming too.'

Ned saw the look on Jess's face and knew there was no point arguing with her when she looked like that; she was just like her mother. Nevertheless, in her state of health, with her lungs, he was not going to let her traipse behind Bracken to wherever he might lead them. Scooping her up quickly in his arms, he lifted his daughter onto the horse and told her to grab Bracken's mane while he took hold of the horse's halter.

They set off wondering where Bracken would lead them, Jess excited after all this time to be finally up on his back. She couldn't help wishing it was without her dad holding on to him. Moments later, she got her wish.

Ned released his grip on Bracken's halter as he unlatched the white gate. It swung open and Bracken rushed forward through the opening and galloped off down the field. Ned shouted after them, 'Jess hang on, hang on!'

Jess, thrilled, needed no telling. Bracken's black glossy mane was already wrapped round her hands and, with her legs pressed firmly into his flanks, Jess could not remember the last time she had felt so happy. They flew past the nervous Molly and, with the mighty power of the horse beneath her, Jess thought she was in heaven.

Bracken slowed to a walk and Jess made out the slumped form of the little fawn as they approached. Jess really didn't want to get down from Bracken, she could have sat on him all night, but she could tell the animal in front of her was hurt. She jumped down, knelt by the fawn's side and saw the steel shaft and bloody wound. 'Poor little thing,' she sighed, taking off her dressing gown and laying it gently over the young deer.

She sat back on her heels wondering what else she could do, talking softly to reassure the creature as Bracken lowered his head over her shoulder. 'So this is what you wanted us to find boy, was it? Good boy, good boy,' Jess whispered, stroking Bracken's cheek.

Ned arrived on the scene, puffing and panting. He stood for a moment, hands on hips, trying to catch his breath, looking down at Jess and the dressing-gown-covered shape beside her with the fawn's head poking out.

Jess looked up at her dad. 'It's a young deer, Dad. It's hurt. There's something sticking out of its neck.'

'Let me have a look, love.' Ned bent down and placed the flat of his palm gently on top of the fawn's head, hoping to keep her still and prevent further injury. He drew back the dressing gown carefully. The clouds parted and the escaping moonlight lit up the steel bolt sticking out of the fawn's neck.

Ned considered what to do for the best, one hand still restraining the fawn. He spoke quietly so as not to frighten the deer. 'Jess, this is what we are going to do. Firstly, I'm going to move your dressing gown up and cover the deer's head with it. This will help keep the little thing calm, not seeing all us big daft 'uns round it. Then I'm going to take Bracken and nip back to t'farm sharpish. I'll hitch Bracken up to t'wagon and I'll be back down here in no time at all. While I'm gone, you place your hand where I've got mine and try and keep her as calm as you can and not let her wriggle about. Is that okay? I won't be long.'

'But what are you going to do with the deer when you come back, Dad?' Jess asked, fearing the worst.

'Put it in t'back of the wagon. Can't have t'poor thing lying here sufferin' all night. Then I'll take it back up to the barn where there's a bit more light and see if there is anything more can be done for it.'

Ned's words reassured Jess but, as a farmer's daughter, she knew if animals were badly injured sometimes the only thing you could do with them – and the kindest thing – was to put them out of their misery. She did not want the fawn to die; it was only a baby and had just started out on its life. 'Okay, Dad, but hurry on back, won't you?'

'We'll be back before you know it,' said Ned, jumping up onto Bracken.

As Ned rode into the farmyard and dismounted, Christine shouted over from the front door, 'What's going on?'

'Young deer lying injured in the horses' field. I'm going to hitch up a wagon and bring it on up to the barn, see if I can do anything with it.'

'Where's Jess? You've not left her down there on her own, have you?'

'Yes. Don't worry, she'll be fine. It's only a tiny fawn, smaller than a lamb, it is.'

'Why didn't you just carry it up then, instead of leaving Jess down there all on her own?'

'It crossed me mind, love, but I think it'll be kinder to put t'little creature in t'back of t'wagon. I'm not too sure how badly injured it is and I don't want t'creature suffering more than necessary if I can help it.'

'All right,' replied Christine. 'But I don't like leaving Jess down there on her own. Come on, hurry up. I'll give you a hand.' Together they hitched Bracken to the wagon.

The wagon rolled to a stop by the fawn. Christine got down and put her arm round Jess as Ned carefully lifted the small animal onto the back of the wagon. He asked Christine to stay beside it. Jess wanted to be with the fawn too and, after helping both of them up onto the back, Ned went round to the front of the wagon, picked up the reins and called to Bracken, 'Move on, boy, move on.'

Ned stopped the wagon by the front door to let Christine and Jess get off. 'Best you two go inside and get back to bed. Leave me to look after the fawn now.'

'But Dad, I want to come with you. You might need my help.'

'Now, Jess, get down from the wagon,' Christine said firmly. 'Leave the deer to your father. We have your health to think about as well as that poor little creature's. You've had enough excitement for one day and you need your sleep.'

'But Mum…'

'Don't "but Mum" me nothing, Jess. Inside with you now and leave the deer to your dad. He will see to it. Now up to bed with you this minute.'

'But Dad…' pleaded Jess.

'Don't you be bringing your father into this,' warned Christine. 'Come on, get down off the wagon and go upstairs to bed. What would the doctor say if he knew we were letting you stay out till this time and you were not getting your sleep?'

Jess reluctantly climbed down from the wagon. She stood in the yard and asked one last time, 'Do you think the fawn will be all right, Dad?'

'Well, we'll have to wait and see. Never can tell how wild animals will be. Off inside and up them stairs with you now.'

As Jess and Christine went inside, Ned moved Bracken to the barn. The fawn did not stir as he laid it gently down on the straw-covered floor. He left it there as he lit the oil lamp and returned to have a closer look at the young animal.

His attention focused straight away on the steel bolt sticking out from its neck. Ned felt sick, not from the sight of the bolt and the bloody wound but from the knowledge of his own stupidity. He realised it must have been Billy and Ralph who shot the deer. How stupid could he have been? Instead of checking the boys more thoroughly, he had put money and his own worries before the safety of the two young boys. Seeing the bolt made him realise they could have seriously hurt or even killed one another, as well as damaging this magnificent creature.

He bent down further to help the little deer but the spark of life had disappeared from its eyes.

Ned cleaned and hung the deer from a peg in the barn and put out the lamp. As he crossed the yard to the house, he thought he would take the fawn over to Mrs Robinson's tomorrow. She could make a few venison pies out of it and, at the same time, he would have a word with her about Billy, Ralph, and her late husband's crossbow. He would let her know Billy had hold of it and could do some serious harm. Ask her to have a word with him and take the thing off him. He was certain she would see sense; what mother wouldn't?

In the morning, as they were sitting round the kitchen table having breakfast, Ned told Jess he had made the little fawn as comfortable as he could but unfortunately there was nothing more he could do to save it. The poor little creature had passed away. To Ned's surprise, Jess did not seem too upset at the news; that was because she had something more important on her mind.

When Ned stopped speaking, Jess looked thoughtfully from one parent to the other. 'Dad, Mum, do you know what Bracken did last night?'

'Of course we do, pet,' replied Christine. By this time Ned was tucking into his breakfast, had his mouth full and could not join in the conversation.

'No, I mean do you *really* know what Bracken did last night?'

'Yes, love, we do. He tried to help the poor little fawn,' replied Christine.

'But have you thought about just what he did?'

'Well he came and got us and...' Then Christine stopped and fell silent as the penny dropped and it dawned on her exactly what Jess was getting at.

'Exactly,' said Jess, seeing the knowledge register on her mum's face. 'Bracken came and knocked on the door. Mum, Dad, Bracken knocked on the door!'

Ned almost choked on his food. He hadn't given it a thought until then but yes, Jess was right. Now he came to think about it, it was the loud banging on the door that had woken them all up. Who else could have banged on the door? When he had opened it, only Bracken was there. The room fell silent; even Ned's loud chomping ceased as he gulped down his food and his mouth fell open.

The three of them sat around the table, deep in thought about what the horse had done. Not one of them had seen Bracken; they could only guess at how he had knocked on the door the previous night.

Chapter 23
I HEARD HIM KNOCK ONCE

WITH THE LOAN money from the bank dwindling away and little other income, working life on the farm became unbearable. Ned struggled on, always with one eye watching the money, scrimping to save a penny here and a halfpenny there, constantly cutting back on purchasing tools and materials without which jobs were more difficult and took twice as long. It was inevitable the farm should suffer. After all the years of hard work by Ned's family, his father and mother, his father's father before that, seeing the farm fail did not rest easily on Ned's shoulders. He blamed himself, yet knew he was blameless. The decline of the farm was just another sign of the times.

Stressed, tired, overworked and at his wits' end with worry, he was irritable and short-tempered and far from his normal self. He knew his moods upset Christine and Jess and tried for their sakes not to show his fear but at times his true feelings slipped out; he was not fooling anyone.

No matter his own stress, though, Ned never forgot that there were others, many others in this recession far worse off than he was. It increased his frustration and saddened him further that he was too busy seeing to the needs of his own family to spare the time to lend those less fortunate a hand. This feeling of helplessness and inadequacy added to his disquiet. He would often despair, head held in cupped hands. 'What is humanity coming to when you can't help a fellow man in need?'

Nevertheless there were moments, even during these desperate times, when the recession and the misery it wrought were put to one side and temporarily forgotten. These moments were found within the comfort of his family, more often than not in the kitchen or at meal times when they discussed the horse Bracken and his exploits, particularly with the fawn. Led usually by Jess, talk of Bracken gave them something else to think about and lent a welcome distraction from their concerns and fears. However, as welcome as these brief respites were from cruel reality, even they were to end.

Ned and Christine were once again disturbed from their slumbers in the middle of the night. This time it was not Bracken knocking at the door or any other outside noise that roused them; it was the sound of Jess's harsh coughing. Christine got out of bed to go and see to her daughter. Ned lit the lamp on the bedside table and carried it through, following his wife across the landing.

When they entered Jess's bedroom, they saw their daughter labouring for breath, her nightclothes soaked with perspiration. She was heaving into a white handkerchief clutched in front of her mouth. The handkerchief, embroidered with a garland of roses, was covered in blood.

Christine knew straight away that it was something serious. 'Ned, quick, go and fetch the doctor.'

Ned didn't bother to reply; he could see Jess's condition plainly. He handed the lamp to Christine and left immediately. Christine put the lamp down by the side of the bed and wrapped her arms round Jess, whispering softly in her daughter's ear that everything would be all right.

Ned hurried back to their bedroom. His shirt and trousers were lying on the floor. He pulled up his trousers, grabbed his shirt and headed out of the door. He was putting his arm into the shirtsleeve when he tripped and fell, rolling down the stairs. He reached out to break his fall but his fingers found only fresh air. Rolling and tumbling, he desperately tried to grab hold of something but then his head met the hard limestone at the bottom of the stairs. His skull cracked open like a soft-boiled egg hit with a silver spoon, spilling blood and cerebral fluid over the floor.

Christine did not hear Ned tumble; Jess's paroxysm of coughing masked any noise. Nor did she hear her husband call for help because he did not. Ned lay in a broken heap at the foot of the stairs, dead.

Oblivious to Ned's plight, her arms round Jess, Christine helped her daughter to sit up, hoping it would make her more comfortable and help relieve her coughing. The coughing eased but not for long.

Throughout the night, Christine did her best to soothe and support her daughter. Nothing she did seemed to have much effect. Jess continued to struggle for breath, coughing and bringing up blood. Christine had replaced the bloodstained hanky with a new one but this was now wet with blood. She gave Jess another fresh hanky and wondered what was taking Ned so long; surely he should have been back with the doctor by now!

Chapter 24
BACK TO THE LAND

As DAWN BROKE, daylight came creeping about the house.

Jess let go of her blood-splattered handkerchief, her hands clutching at her chest as she struggled for breath. Christine embraced her, feeling her child's pain. 'Oh where, where can Ned be?' she repeated silently to herself.

Suddenly she felt Jess spasm, lurch forward; blood spewed from the girl's mouth, spattering the bedcovers. Christine watched helplessly as her daughter struggled; she watched helplessly, unable to stop the gush of blood; she watched as her beloved child choked to death in her arms.

Christine would never know how long she sat there rocking back and forth, clutching her lifeless daughter's body, sobbing, heartbroken. She wanted Ned beside her, to hear the tenderness of his voice; she wanted him there to bring her daughter back.

Christine would never recall how long she clung to Jess before she released her and laid her daughter's body down on the bed, her head resting upon the pillow. Neither would she ever remember getting up, leaning over Jess, caressing her daughter's hair and sweeping aside the few wispy strands that had fallen across her child's sweet face, or kissing her daughter one last time before she left the room. She would never remember walking to the stairs – but she would never forget looking down and seeing the horror of

Ned's grotesquely twisted body.

Screaming wildly, she ran down the stairs and flung herself beside her husband. She shook and pummelled him, shouting, 'Ned, get up! Get up Ned, wake up! Get up!' Her shouts drowned out the knocking at the door.

Ned's mother found them that morning. Up early, a habit borne from a lifetime of living on the farm, she had come to call, have a social and catch up on the news, as she put it. It was something she tried to do as often as her ageing bones would allow. Ned was usually out, busy on the farm, so she never really got chance to see as much of him as she would have liked. Nevertheless, she enjoyed her time with the girls, as she referred to Christine and Jess; as she was getting older, she thought it was good to spend time in the company of young folks, it made her feel alive.

As she sauntered along the lane up to the farm, an odd feeling came over her. She sensed that something was not right. She saw the horses through the hedgerow, in the field; both were skittish. She knew Molly could get a bit jittery at times but Bracken never; he was as brave as a lion. To see Bracken nervous sent a shiver down her old spine.

Nearing the farmhouse, she heard the tormented wailing. She hurried on up to the door and knocked; no one answered. She could hear clearly the pitiful cries from within. She knocked louder, more urgently, but again there was no answer. She opened her bag and pulled out her purse in which she kept a key to the house. 'No point waiting outside in the cold, Mum, if we don't hear you knocking. Just you let yourself in with this,' Ned had told her when he handed her the spare key.

She put the key in the lock, opened the door and stopped dead in her tracks, staring at the sight that greeted her. Her son was slumped at the bottom of the stairs in a pool of blood; Christine knelt over him, head upon his chest, fists pummelling his lifeless body, screaming for him to wake up. The old woman sank to her knees. The sense of her presence jolted Christine and brought her back to her senses. She stopped screaming and beating Ned but continued sobbing desperately.

The two women remained by Ned's body for an interval in which they had no sense of time. The old woman was unable to speak, her thoughts swirling, sentimental, self-reproaching, heartbreaking, a fog inside her head as Christine sobbed. She remembered the baby she had once fed, the boy that Nathanial and she had raised, the man they had moulded. She knew with more sadness than she could bear that she was oh so proud of the man her son had become. Yet she had never told him. Now she never would.

Lesser women would have screamed or fainted at what confronted her as she opened the door but Ned's mother had been a farmer's wife, a soldier's wife, a hardy, practical woman who had dealt with her fair share in her time. A little strength returned, as did her voice. She said quietly to Christine, 'Tell me, dear, what happened?'

Christine lifted her head from Ned's chest and whispered through her tears, 'Jess is dead. Ned must have slipped and fallen when I sent him to fetch the doctor.' Unable to say more, she bent her head, once again covering Ned with her tears.

The old woman tried to get up off the limestone floor. Her joints creaked as she straightened up and stepped over Ned's legs. She was feeble and she struggled but wearily she climbed the stairs and went into Jess's bedroom. She saw her granddaughter, eyes open, the bloodstained sheet drawn up beneath her chin.

Tears trickled down the old woman's face. She forced herself over to the cupboard, removed two clean sheets and ripped the bloody one off Jess. She bundled it up and threw it into a corner of the bedroom, closed Jess's eyes, then laid a clean sheet over her granddaughter's body and pulled it up over her face. She looked down at Jess and said, 'Good night, my little angel.' She could say no more; she knew that if she did, she would break down completely and she could not afford to do that. She still had to see to her son and Christine.

She went back downstairs and rested her hand on Christine's shoulder. 'Come on, Christine,' she said softly. 'You must get up now. Help me cover Ned.'

The two women placed the second sheet over Ned's body and stood looking down until the old woman took hold of Christine's hand and spoke again. 'Come along, we can do no more. We'll sit in the kitchen until we are ready, then we'll go and inform the authorities.'

Christine nodded numbly and together they walked into the kitchen.

✕ ✕ ✕

Christine went to live with her mother-in-law in her cottage on the edge of town. After a simple ceremony, Ned and Jess were buried together in a small plot on the farm. The farm and livestock were put up for sale; the estate agent said it would be difficult to sell the property under the present financial climate and suggested that it would be prudent if the livestock were sold off separately in order to keep costs as low as possible. He said he would arrange for someone to look after the animals in the meantime.

Chapter 25
SOLD

OVER THE COMING days Bracken watched as men put up the 'For Sale' sign at the top of the lane. He watched and his ears pricked up when a gaily painted caravan drew in and stopped. He watched as the dark-haired driver, the reins still held in his hand, stood up on the wagon and peered over the hedgerow. He watched as the man stared at him, inspecting him – and didn't like it.

Bracken's ears went back, and he bared his teeth and reared up, irritated at the man's glare.

'So you don't like me, eh,' shouted the gypsy. 'We'll soon see about that.'

The gypsy sat down and drove up to the farmhouse. In the farmyard, he found the man appointed to look after the livestock by the selling agent. They agreed a price and money changed hands. The transaction complete, the gypsy and the agent walked down to the white gate to get the horse.

The gypsy and the agent barely managed to handle the skittish and contrary Bracken. They pulled and manhandled him out of the field until finally they got him into the yard and tethered him to the back of the caravan. Having securely fastened Bracken, the gypsy jumped on board then he made a wide turn in the farmyard and went back down the lane, turned right at the bottom and took the road into town.

Tied behind the caravan, Bracken was edgy. The shape of the gypsy's caravan with its tall sides and round roof was strange but it was not this or being roped to the caravan that made Bracken uneasy. Ned had often tied young Bracken to the back of a wagon to get him used to it. No, it was something the horse sensed about the dark-haired man that put him on edge. Nevertheless, by the time they reached the outskirts of town Bracken had settled.

The gypsy drove through the town centre. In this time of recession, the politicians had imposed cutbacks on civic spending. The shortfall in council money was evident in the grubby appearance of the streets and main buildings. The town hall, once so grand with its neat sandstone forecourt, flowerbeds, lawns and attractive display of well-cared-for hanging baskets, looked dirty and unkempt. Weeds filled the flowerbeds, yellow patches of moss covered the lawns and only dry, withered stalks hung limp over the sides of the wicker baskets.

Men loitered about the dirty streets, a common sight now that unemployment was so high. The jobless paced up and down drearily, wearing their worn and patched clothes, flat caps pulled down over their faces but unable still to conceal their hopeless plight and feelings of worthlessness. It was as if the two animals, the one pulling the caravan and Bracken tied behind, felt their utter despair. Both horses trudged through the streets of the town with their heads drooping, their ears flattened.

About half a mile on the other side of town, Bracken caught the trace of a pungent smell hanging in the air. The stench grew stronger the further they went, attacking the back of his throat. They continued, soon coming upon a rambling set of red-bricked, single storey buildings in the centre of which stood a tall, round chimney stack built out of the same red brick. Thick clouds of acrid smoke belched out from the top of the chimney.

The gypsy turned the caravan off the road through the open, iron-spiked gates into the factory yard. He pulled to a halt in front of two large, green sliding doors. Above the doors there was a hole in the building from which a gantry beam extended over the yard. At one end of the beam hung a chain hoist attached to a wheeled trolley that enabled the hoist to travel up and down the length of the beam.

The gypsy tied the reins round the brake handle and jumped down from the caravan. He walked up to the horse at the front, released the caravan shafts and unbuckled the harness. He took off the horse's bridle and laid it down between his feet. He brought the horse forward until it was well clear of the shafts before going back inside the caravan. Seconds later he came out holding a rifle, walked up to the unharnessed horse, held the rifle to its head and shot it.

As the gun went off, at the sight of the dead horse, Bracken reared. The tether about him tightened and his mighty strength lifted the caravan, causing it to lurch, lift off the ground and come crashing back down. He reared again, lifting the wagon as he rose, and once more the caravan crashed down and swayed from side to side. Frantic, Bracken climbed up on his powerful hind legs; again the caravan smashed down to the ground, rocking and rolling. Something came loose from the wagon and fell underneath it, away to one side. It was a metal locking pin. As it fell out, a door at the back of the caravan, cleverly painted and disguised, flipped open to reveal a secret compartment.

Seeing the concealed door open, the gypsy acted quickly. As Bracken landed, he hit the horse full in the face with the butt of the rifle, almost knocking Bracken out cold. Having sorted out the horse, the gypsy bent down, picked up the fallen pin and looked around shiftily to make sure no one had seen. He closed the compartment door and, reaching under the wagon, quickly refitted the locking pin.

The gypsy checked again, making doubly sure no one had noticed the secret panel. Satisfied, he came round and again took his rifle to Bracken, hitting him so hard that the horse's legs buckled. It was all Bracken could do to remain standing.

By this time the few workers in the factory, hearing the rifle shot, noise and commotion outside, rushed to see what the ruckus was all about. They slid back one of the green doors but by the time it was open, all was calm. The gypsy, spying the peeking workers, lost no time in tackling them.

He approached one of the men aggressively and pointed to the body of the dead horse. 'I've done a deal with your boss man an' been paid for the horse. Now you hook it up and take it so I can get other horse between shafts and be on my way.'

The gypsy looked brutally on the spiritless faces of the workers; they reminded him of rabbits caught in lamplight waiting for the poacher to pull the trigger. 'Come on, shift yourselves and move bloody carcass or I tell your boss what bunch of lazy good-for-nothings he has working for him.'

Hearing mention of their boss and in fear of losing their jobs, the men moved like the exploited and fearful creatures they were.

A man wearing blood-smeared brown overalls put a couple of leather straps round the dead horse and attached the hook and chain. Another man worked the hoist; the chain rattled as he took up the slack and the carcass was dragged across the yard. Underneath the beam, the horse started to lift off the ground. The man kept working the hoist until the horse's lifeless legs dangled freely above the ground. Then both men slid the green doors fully open and pushed the dead animal inside.

The gypsy waited until all the men were back in the glue factory and the sliding doors were firmly shut once more. He rechecked the locking pin of the secret compartment, ensuring it was properly in place, then untied Bracken, gripped his halter and pulled the still dazed and unsteady horse to the front of the caravan. The gypsy picked up the collar and put it round Bracken's neck, threw the harness over his back, fastened the buckles tightly and backed him up between the caravan's shafts.

Chapter 26
MINE ALL MINE

ONCE AGAIN, THE Peculiar Man could not believe his luck. The insider dealing had paid off very handsomely indeed.

As foretold by his cronies at his wife's funeral, a large company was expanding and acquiring other businesses to add to its already extensive portfolio. The Peculiar Man had invested substantially, buying shares in the smaller companies well before negotiations for their acquisition became public knowledge; thus he acquired them at an extremely attractive price.

Once the open market heard about the takeover, the share price rocketed as investors saw them as a sure-fire bet and rushed to buy. The Peculiar Man sold his shares and made a considerable profit. In the process he didn't even have to move out of his favourite armchair; he certainly didn't come anywhere near breaking into a sweat or dirtying his hands, and he certainly did not think anything he had done was criminal. His friends were all directors of the companies concerned and what are friends for, if not to help one another?

At the same time as he made the extortionately large sum of money selling his recently acquired shares, word reached his ear that the commoner's farm was up for sale. Just how lucky could he be? The Peculiar Man rubbed his hands in glee. He had heard something trite regarding the farmer and his young daughter; she had died of some illness or what have you and the farmer in some kind of an accident. What did he care about such a trivial matter as how they died? What was important was that now he could acquire the farm. He had, as he put it, ample spare change to purchase the property. Finally, after all this time, the estate would once again be complete and all his.

The Peculiar Man summoned his estate manager and gave him instructions to see the agent in charge of the sale, find out the price and report back without delay.

The estate manager rode into town, found the selling agent's business premises and discussed matters according to the Peculiar Man's instructions. The estate manager was back in front of the Peculiar Man within three hours, informing him of the asking price for the farm. The Peculiar Man thought the price very reasonable indeed. However, turning his back on the manager, he pondered. Times were hard, or so he kept hearing, and in hard times who was going to have that sort of money to buy the farm? No one round these parts, that was for sure. The Peculiar Man thought he might be able to purchase the farm for a pittance. As far as he was concerned, he was only buying back land that rightfully belonged to the estate.

He made up his mind; he would offer a trifle, chance his arm. After all, so far this had been his lucky year!

The Peculiar Man turned round to the estate manager and addressed him. 'This is the price I will pay for the entire farm, lock stock and barrel.' He detailed his price and terms. The estate manager could not help grimacing; the amount fell miserably short of the asking price.

The Peculiar Man ignored the manager's expression; he thought that the man might have indigestion problems through not eating sufficient fruit compote. He continued, 'You can have half a per cent for yourself of anything you manage to negotiate below that figure.' That should be more than enough incentive for him, the Peculiar Man thought. He added: 'Do not come back here without securing the purchase. Buy the farm for more than the price I've said, however, then your job will be on the line and I might have to look round for someone more competent to fill your position. Do you understand?'

The Peculiar Man did not wait for a reply, which was just as well as the estate manager was rendered speechless. Dismissing the manager with a wave of his hand, the Peculiar Man sent him on his way back into town.

The estate manager, still dumbfound when he dismounted his horse, walked back into the selling agent's office. He informed the agent of the Peculiar Man's miserly price but, being an ethical man, he did not attempt to negotiate a lesser price and earn anything for himself. Unlike the Peculiar Man, the manager had no intention of cheating Christine. He'd had dealings with the Bradshaws and, in his humble opinion, Christine and Ned were honest, hard-working folk. Past business between him and Ned had always been carried out in good accord.

The selling agent's face fell when he heard the offer and he responded, 'I couldn't possibly sell the property for that price.'

The manager, remembering the Peculiar Man's threat that his job was at risk, continued with the negotiation. 'What is the lowest price you would accept?'

The selling agent was fully aware of the adverse times in which they lived. He had not sold a property for months and desperately needed the commission this sale would afford him; he lowered the asking price but it was still considerably higher than the price offered by the Peculiar Man.

In his position, the estate manager had the authority to accept the agent's reduced price. He knew, however, that it was a risk and he would be putting his job at stake. The estate manager, an honourable man, thought: 'To hell with it! I've been through and seen worse. I'll be dammed if I'm going to stand by and see a bereaved woman swindled out of a fair deal! Hasn't Christine suffered enough losing her husband and daughter?'

The estate manager accepted the agent's revised offer, shook on the deal and signed the papers giving permission for the transaction to proceed and the sale to go through. He would deal with the repercussions later. As he signed the legal documents, he thought: 'Damn the Peculiar Man! Let him do his worst. Let him dismiss me. I'm at an age where I should have retired and hung up my boots years ago.'

The estate manager rode back to the manor at a leisurely pace, far more relaxed than when he departed. He felt contented and at peace. He had his horse taken care of and walked from the stables through the courtyard to see the Peculiar Man. He met him in the study and told him the price he had paid for Bradshaw's farm. He added that he also signed the legal papers to avoid any unnecessary delay so the deal could be concluded before another interested bidder came on the scene and possibly raised the price.

The Peculiar Man nodded and said, 'I see.' Then he dismissed the manager with a wave of his hand.

The Peculiar Man knew his previous threat about the estate manager's job was an empty one. He could not run the estate without him. Nevertheless, he would keep a careful eye on his manager from now on. It didn't do to let the underlings start making decisions and thinking for themselves. What sort of place would the world be if that happened? He dreaded to think.

THE STORY: PART TWO

Chapter 27
A LAUGHABLE PROBLEM

THE PECULIAR MAN had just finished performing what had become his monthly deed. It was a deed he did not enjoy and afterwards he departed from his wife's boudoir as quickly as possible and returned to the sanctuary of his own bedroom. There, lying on the bed with his hands by his sides, he gazed up at the ornate plaster ceiling rose and mulled over the situation. He had a problem: his wife.

The Peculiar Man and Lady Elora had been married for nearly two years and, in his mind, things were working out far better than expected. That was part of the problem. He certainly did not love the woman or, for that matter, have any genuine feelings for her but she was company and they had several things in common. To the Peculiar Man's relief, one of those was she did not show any enthusiasm for the sexual act. She often said she did not enjoy it and found the mechanics ludicrous. 'Fit only for dogs in the street,' was an expression she used after the monthly copulation. She partook only because of her neediness for a child.

The Peculiar Man had wed for the single purpose of producing an heir. After two years of marriage, his wife showed no signs of delivering one. The Peculiar Man considered this totally unacceptable for a lady of breeding; he would have expected her to have the decency to get in the family way by now. However, she seemed as enthusiastic for a child as he was, so was she solely to blame?

The Peculiar Man wrestled with the question: was she solely to blame? After much deliberation, he reached the conclusion that of course she was. How could a male of his high standing and noble lineage not produce anything other than high-quality seed? It would be a crime against nature for such a man as he to be infertile. God would never allow such a thing, he reasoned. So he concluded that she was the problem – but what to do about her? Should he resort to his previous scheme or was there another option? As his mind wrestled to find solutions, he fell asleep.

The Peculiar Man woke early the next morning, still without answers. He lay on his fine feather mattress, snug and warm under laundered cotton sheets. Problems, problems, he thought. Why was life so hard? But he was not going to lie in bed all morning upsetting himself; he had other matters to see to. He would address the issue of his wife at a more convenient time and certainly not let it spoil the rest of his day.

He had planned his day already. First on the agenda was a hearty breakfast, afterwards a jolly ride round the estate on his favourite horse, then a spot of luncheon. Perhaps a snooze in the library once he had dined then later in the evening he would change into suitable attire and get the chauffer to drive him to his club, where he would catch up with his chums. A night with his contemporaries always did him good and helped him to see things more clearly.

Later that day the Peculiar Man's black Bentley pulled up alongside the curb directly in front of the short flight of steps leading from the pavement to the gentlemen's club. The uniformed chauffer jumped out, hurried round the front of the car and opened the rear passenger door. As the Peculiar Man alighted, he looked up and saw a rather rotund man with a mop of grey hair and a large bushy moustache. He was standing at the bottom of the steps wearing a long black overcoat and obviously waiting for him.

'Good evening,' said the Peculiar Man.

'Good evening to you, my boy,' said Lord Rasstone. 'Just on my way up when I saw you arrive. Thought I recognised the car – and how fortunate that I did. I was hoping to bump into you at some point and have a word. No point wasting an opportunity, as the Romans were always fond of saying, overly fond, if you ask me. *Carpe diem*, seize the day. Come, my boy, will you join me for a drink? I promise not to keep you to myself for too long.'

Caught on the hop, the Peculiar Man could not think up an excuse fast enough to refuse his father-in-law's invitation. Spending time with the old duffer was certainly not what he had planned for tonight. As the two men climbed up the steps to the club, the Peculiar Man was already regretting he had not declined Rasstone's invitation. Nevertheless, he resigned himself to having one drink, no more, before excusing himself and slipping away.

At the top of the steps, the concierge held the door open and they walked inside. They entered the lobby where Lord Rasstone casually draped his arm over the Peculiar Man's shoulders and discreetly manoeuvred him away from the club bar, along the teardrop-chandeliered lobby into the quieter and less crowded members' lounge.

They entered the lounge via an arch adorned with gold cherubs. On the opposite wall were three windows, the middle window larger than those on either side, each draped with heavy velvet curtains. The curtains, closed at this hour, helped to keep the heat in and the cold of the night out, along with any prying eyes on the street. Green leather armchairs and matching sofas were scattered around the room. Rasstone ignored these and led the Peculiar Man to an unoccupied table with two carver chairs in the far corner of the room, next to the left-hand window.

When they were seated, a waiter came over and enquired if

they would like a drink. 'Scotch and ice for me, Wilfred. That okay for you, my boy?' Lord Rasstone enquired. The Peculiar Man nodded his consent.

'Make that two scotches, my man,' said Rasstone to the long-serving waiter.

Rasstone and the Peculiar Man exchanged small talk until Wilfred returned with two tumblers of scotch, served the drinks and retreated out of earshot, allowing them to talk freely without fear of being overheard.

Lord Rasstone cleared his throat and took a small sip of his drink before introducing the purpose of their meeting. 'Ah, just the ticket. Can't beat a drop of scotch on a cold night. Now, my boy, my good lady wife who has to be obeyed, asked me if I could have a discreet word with you.'

Hearing Rasstone's words, the Peculiar Man looked perplexed. He sat back, wondering what this conversation was going to be about.

Lord Rasstone continued, 'None of us are getting any younger and I should know, what…' He laughed. 'As time is marching on for Lady Rasstone, she feels it would be nice if we could spend a little time with our grandchildren. The trouble is, old boy, we haven't got any. And what with you being wed to our only child for the past two years...' Here Rasstone paused, took up the tumbler and had another sip of his scotch before resuming. 'Well, as I was saying, two years have passed by and Lady Rasstone was wondering if you are experiencing any difficulties on the home front, so to speak. If so, is there any way in which the two of us could help? We don't want to interfere between man and wife, just want to help out if we can. I know Lady Rasstone will most certainly have a delicate word in our daughter's ear on your behalf, should you so wish.'

My God, thought the Peculiar Man, the impertinence of the damned fellow. If it wasn't for his barren daughter, they could

144

have had one or possibly two sprogs running round biting their ankles by now. If only Rasstone and his wife knew how many times he'd had to steel himself and gird his loins in the call of duty. Thinking about it made the Peculiar Man shudder.

'Well,' continued Lord Rasstone, feeling a little uncomfortable, 'I wondered if you could give it some thought. If there is anything, anything at all that we can do, then don't be shy to ask. After all, we are family.'

The Peculiar Man masked his outrage at what he took as an affront to his manhood and simply replied, 'I take on board what you say and will discuss it with my wife.' Then, throwing back his scotch, he said curtly, 'Now if you'll excuse me, I've arranged to meet some of my associates in the members' bar and I'm already late. I'll bid you good evening.' With that, he got up and walked out of the lounge.

In contrast to the stuffy lounge, the bar, which had been renovated recently in the latest art-deco style, was bright and modern. White mouldings complemented the sharp-edged ceiling that was made of coloured glass; the angularity of the wall lights served to highlight the slender curves of the ornate table lamps, moulded in the shape of women, placed about the room.

The Peculiar Man did not have to look hard to find his cronies; five of them were at the end of the bar. Two were seated on chrome bar stools while the other three were standing. All were talking animatedly and it was plain to see that they had already consumed a few stiff drinks.

The Peculiar Man was greeted with handshakes and, 'What are you for, old sport?' by one of the seated men.

'Scotch will do nicely thank you,' he replied. 'Sorry I'm late, chaps. Father-in-law collared me on the way in. Wanted to talk to me about making him and his dotty old wife grandparents, would you believe? Basically, he said it's about time I had kids and all that malarkey. You know, do the business so to speak.

Damn cheek of the man.'

One of the standing men piped up good-humouredly, 'Not having any trouble in that department, are we?' The others laughed.

Someone passed the Peculiar Man his drink; he took a large swallow as the man, the mirth disappearing from his face, continued speaking in a more sober vain. 'Seriously though, if you are keen, I have a sure-fire remedy.' The Peculiar Man put down his glass, interest showing in his face.

'Ah,' the man resumed, 'I see you are. Well, if you want to get a woman with child, the first thing you must remember is that the fair sex are moody creatures. It is, therefore, imperative to get them in the right mood. The best way to do this, so I'm reliably informed, is firstly get one of the servants to draw a warm bath. You make sure the bath has plenty of soapy bubbles, scented water and, for good measure, sprinkle in some rose petals. Next, escort the lady of your desire to the bathroom. Whisper sweet nothings in her ear while gently caressing and tenderly undressing her as you guide her into the bath. Once you have seen her comfortably settled, leave the bathroom. That's right, you heard me: leave the bathroom and your intended conquest to her own devices, to relax and pamper herself.'

The Peculiar Man was taking all he heard very seriously, making mental notes; it had never crossed his mind to do anything remotely like this.

The speaker raised his glass to his lips and took another quick sip of his drink before putting it down and continuing. 'As she luxuriates in the warm water, relaxing amid the foam and heady aroma of rose petals, go to her boudoir. Lay the scanty, expensive lingerie that you had the foresight to purchase in readiness for this night upon her pillow.'

The Peculiar Man listened with rapt attention.

'After about an hour, knock gently on the bathroom door and

softly whisper that you have left a surprise on her bed. Being a woman and by nature inquisitive, she won't be able to help herself; her impulsive nature will compel her to get out of the bath. Once she has dried her delicate skin, she will tiptoe naked to her bedroom to see what you have left there. Immediately her eyes fall on the lingerie, her passion will be inflamed, she won't be able to resist slipping on the lacy garments. And when she does, ah, when she does… The combination of hot, scented water, the erotic feel of the delicate material against her skin, it will be too much. Her body will tingle, she will be moist and warm, her pretty head will fill with lust and amorous thoughts. Now here is the most important part.'

The man paused and took his time as he brought his glass to his lips. He sipped, licked his lips and slowly placed the glass back down upon the bar. The Peculiar Man could hardly wait for him to tell them what the important part was; he also picked up his tumbler but there was nothing sensual whatsoever in the way he gulped back his scotch.

The man turned his head and slowly looked, one by one, into the faces of his chums. The last person he gazed upon was the Peculiar Man. 'Now,' the man said, 'now, the really important part.' He raised his hand, caressed his chin slowly, a look of uncertainty upon his face, pondering; should he reveal this intimate secret or not? You could hear a pin drop. His expression changed as if he had made his mind up and would let them in on it. Speaking in barely more than a whisper he continued, 'When she is scantily clad in the bedroom, leave her alone. On no account go into her room.'

His voiced dropped even lower. 'I repeat, do not go in to her. Instead, make your way downstairs to the servants' quarters. Once you're there, get hold of your youngest and fastest servant.'

The Peculiar Man could hardly contain himself; he took another quick swallow of scotch, desperately needing to know what happened next. Suddenly, the man's voice rose and, laughing, he shouted out. 'Tell him to come and fetch me!'

The cronies hooted and hollered; they thought it hilarious. The Peculiar Man did not. He slammed his glass down on the bar, turned and abruptly walked out of the club.

The Peculiar Man was livid; first Rasstone and now his chums. His mind seethed. It seemed as if they were all ganging up on him, turning him into a laughing stock. How dare they cast aspersions on his manhood! He had no interest in sex, he wasn't dirty, sordid and depraved like they were; he was above that, he was clean, noble and pure. He would show them he was a real man. Yes, he would take something from their foolish jape. He would get one of the servants to fetch somebody all right but it wouldn't be that clown! He would fetch someone all right!

Arriving back at his stately manor, the Peculiar Man rang for Jarvis.

Chapter 28
BACK ON COURSE

IT WAS A special time in the gypsy calendar. For a night and a day, they would drink, make merry and, of course, there would be the women and the dogs. They were gathering now in large numbers, coming from far and wide to attend the festivities. Some came in processions of two, three and four caravans, turning off the lane and driving through the open gate into the meadow. Others, like the dark-haired gypsy, came alone. But come they did, arriving at all hours throughout the day and night.

By late afternoon on the eve of the celebration, all that were going to come had arrived. The pasture was awash in a sea of gaily coloured wagons, a jumble of shapes and sizes and no two the same. Some resembled the dark-haired gypsy's caravan, with tall sides, glass windows and shutters. Others had no windows at all but had rounded sides and a roof constructed of green, maroon or brown canvas. The horses roamed freely about the field, some playing, some sleeping, most grazing; all except for Bracken, secured tightly to the back of the gypsy's caravan by a thick piece of rope.

The gypsy did not like or trust the horse. Since beating Bracken senseless with the butt of his rifle, the horse had been subservient. He had not played up or caused any trouble but the gypsy sensed that the animal was only biding his time and, given half a chance, it would be off. The gypsy had laid out hard cash for the horse and would make damn sure he got his money's worth from the beast before he took it to the knacker's yard and had its bones crushed into glue.

The gypsy knew, though, that today was not a day to be thinking about a horse. Today should be full of thoughts of things to come. Tonight there would be the feast, the wine, the women, and tomorrow the dogs.

The rest of the afternoon passed quickly as preparations for the celebration got underway. By late evening, the aroma of suckling pig turning on spits over the campfires scented the air and the gypsies began to gather, watching the pigskin turn crisp, the fat sizzle and drip onto the flames.

As night fell, tales of daring were told as excited children listened or played round the grown-ups' feet. As darkness truly descended, the little ones fell asleep exhausted and the wine began to flow freely. Then a special time came, a time when the young women, now free from their burdens, came slowly among the revellers and provocatively uncoiled their limbs, igniting male senses already heightened by alcohol. At first, the women's bodies swayed sensually from side to side but later, later under the light of the stars, inhibitions shed, they danced – and how they danced.

Swirling, twirling with gay abandon, their billowing, flowing dresses whirled as the firelight revealed the lustful hunger in their eyes. As their intensity rose, they gyrated, their hot, perspiring bosoms heaving. They flaunted their sex, every one a blur of slender, curvaceous female form. Captivating, enchanting, they spun and danced, weaving their feminine magic into the late hours when one by one, their frenzied passion yearning for release, they singled out their man, a man to satisfy their cravings. Together they ran, disappearing under the cloak of darkness.

The night was a bustle, a blur of feasting, drinking, wild passion and liberation, but the early morning brought activity of a different kind. The gypsy boys and girls were up at first light. They carried sacks and nets and were scampering through the nearby fields and woods; they had hares to catch. The excited children worked in teams, silently creeping up on the cropping animals, surrounding them with their open nets and cutting off any chance of escape. When the hares were caught in the nets, the children plucked them out and held them by their back legs, kicking and wriggling, and dropped them into a sack. By mid morning, the sacks were full and they returned to the camp where they handed them over to the gypsy men. Now the game of hare and dog could begin.

As they made their way towards the event, the effects of the night's festivities showed but nothing would keep them away. Some gypsies held their throbbing heads, others swayed and staggered or cursed and declared that they would never touch drink again, knowing as the words fell off their tongues that it was a promise they would never keep. No matter what state they were in, they managed to get to the site where the dogs and handlers waited.

The dogs were lurchers, cross-breed sight hounds the size of a greyhound but with the tenacity of a terrier. They could smell the hares in the sacks and their excitement grew as, tightly held back, they waited in anticipation, saliva dripping from their jowls.

The black-haired gypsy was there, his caravan upon a small rise. From here he had a good view of proceedings. His word was final in any dispute should argument break out about which dog made the kill. He would also lay down the odds, take the bets, hold the money and pay out to lucky winners. As his caravan was central to proceedings, the event would start from in front of his wagon.

The first dogs to run were displayed. The men ambled up to the caravan and placed their bets then the black-haired gypsy gave a hand signal. Two handlers came forward with their dogs, knelt down on one knee and held their dogs by their collars as a hare was pulled out of a sack and placed on the ground in front of them. An expectant hush fell over the crowd as the hare was released. When it got to the set distance of five dog lengths away, the handlers released their dogs. Uproar broke out as the dogs set off, the gypsies yelling and cursing them on.

Bracken watched from in front of the gypsy's caravan. When he was a young horse, he had teased and chased rabbits in Ned's field but it was nothing like this. Held between the caravan's shafts, he couldn't do anything but watch as hare after hare was ripped to bloody pieces.

The lurchers' speed was frightening but for a time the hare was faster. When the dogs were about to nip the hare's tail, the hare veered off sharply to the right or to the left. The dogs pitched forward, angling their bodies, leaning over as they straightened back in line behind the darting hare. The hare zig-zagged as the dogs were almost upon it, changing direction, and the dogs swerved, bending and twisting in hot slavering pursuit, their noses inches behind their quarry.

The hare darted, ran for its life, but could not keep up the frantic pace. It was bound to tire; you could smell its blood already. Suddenly one of the dogs caught it, hitting its back legs with its snout. The hare flipped over and rolled in mid air. As it came back down, the lurcher was on it. The dog had one of the hare's hind legs in its teeth; you could hear the small bones crack and the hare's loud-pitched squeal as the dog's jaws snapped closed. The hare managed to wriggle free; it took one leap, its broken foot hanging useless, tottered and lay quivering on the ground. The lurcher was on it, had it by the throat, shaking it from side to side. Blood spurted and sprayed the ground as the hare's jugular was ripped open.

The handlers ran out and grabbed their dogs. The losing dog was cursed but the victor walked back proudly, head held high with his dog in tow, the hare firmly in its jaws. Some men went to the wagon to collect their winnings; others milled about the pasture bemoaning their loss. Not one of them paid heed to the trembling Bracken.

The next pair of dogs ran. At the end of this race a lean man, a red felt hat upon his head, wearing a green waistcoat and yellow shirt, pushed his way through the crowd and climbed onto the gypsy's caravan. He stood beside the black-haired gypsy as he paid out on bets and whispered in his ear. The gypsy listened and acknowledged he understood with a nod of the head. The man nodded back then jumped off the caravan, his red felt hat disappearing into the crowd. The gypsy continued to pay the winners; he would attend to the other matter later.

The coursing went on. Hares were brought out of the sacks one by one, wriggling, screaming, and one by one they were run down by the dogs, ripped apart until the sacks were all but empty. At the end of the day, happy at seeing the blood and the violent, cruel deaths, the gypsy men returned to their caravans and women, some with more money than they had come with, others with empty pockets.

Chapter 29
BROTHERS

THE DARK-HAIRED GYPSY waited, as instructed, until late at night before turning his caravan off the road and heading down the drive to the manor. When he got there, Jarvis was waiting by the back door to escort him to the Peculiar Man.

The Peculiar Man sat in his favourite armchair in the drawing room. He let the gypsy stand as he addressed him. 'Our agreement is back on, obviously. I don't want what I ordered last time; some changes are required.' He rose and held out a photograph, saying, 'Get it for me and the rest of the money is yours.'

Without even looking at the photograph, the gypsy took two paces towards the door.

'Damn you, man, where do you think you are going when I'm talking to you?' barked the Peculiar Man.

The gypsy, one hand firmly on the door handle, paused. 'You waste my time. Old deals are old deals, they are dead, finished, forgotten. If you want me not to walk out of the door, if you want me to deliver something for you, then we talk about a new deal. And when I talk, you listen to my price and then you pay all the money up front. You won't cheat me like last time. You may be high and mighty but I know you. You are a cheat, a liar, a thief, a scoundrel just like me. We are the same, you and I. We are so alike we could be brothers.'

The gypsy laughed then his expression changed quickly to menace as he continued. 'Don't try and cheat your brother. You cheat me this time, I will make you pay dearly, have no doubt. You cheat me this time and I will make sure the world knows what you are really like, Mr High and Mighty! Now, brother, you want me to help you or you prefer I walk out the door?'

The Peculiar Man was taken aback; no one had ever threatened him before or spoken to him in such a manner. His mind raced as he saw the public humiliation, the ridicule and fun his cronies would have at his expense. The gypsy started to turn the handle. The Peculiar Man blurted out, 'All right, man, all right. We will make a new deal.'

The gypsy took his hand away from the door. 'It is good that you see sense, my brother. Come, let us sit down like gentlemen and discuss our business.'

The gypsy walked past the Peculiar Man, snatched the photograph from his hand and sat down, making himself comfortable in the Peculiar Man's favourite armchair. The Peculiar Man sat on the sofa opposite, seething.

Settled in the armchair, the gypsy looked at the photograph. It was a picture of Lady Elora, her long black hair brushed to one side of her face. It made his task easier; he knew where to find many girls with black hair. The last wife had auburn hair, which was not so common.

He looked up from the photograph. 'She is pretty, she has a very unusual face. Her likeness will be hard to find. It will cost double what we agreed last time.'

The Peculiar Man stared angrily at the gypsy but knew he had no alternative; he accepted the terms. He went to his study and returned moments later with a roll of money. The gypsy remained seated as the Peculiar Man counted out the white notes into his grubby palm.

Satisfied the money was correct, the gypsy got up. 'I will get word to you when things are ready.' Then, pressing his hand firmly down on the Peculiar Man's shoulder, he said, 'You sit down, brother, make yourself comfortable. I will see myself out.'

The Peculiar Man silently cursed the man once more but the thought of when it all came off...

As Jarvis shut the back door and ensured it was securely locked, the gypsy looked down; he remembered his previous visit and the milk on the doorstep. He bent down and this time, instead of one bottle of gold top, he picked up two. He had a long way to travel; it would take him a few days to reach the coast and the milk would come in handy.

Chapter 30
ROW, ROW, ROW THE BOAT

HE DROVE ON for several miles before turning off and heading down a rutted, overgrown track.

The track ran through the middle of an ancient wood and came out on the other side on a rugged strip of grassland, strewn with boulders. The gypsy steered the caravan warily through the maze of jagged rocks and stopped a few feet away from the cliff's edge, overlooking the sea. Hidden by the old wood, and with a clear view over the ocean for miles around, the gypsy knew no better place to camp and wait.

On the first night there was no let-up in the weather. It continued to rain, the sky laden with heavy cloud, but the gypsy saw no sign of the boat. The weather remained the same the second night but still the boat did not come. On the third night, there was little cloud cover and a full moon shone. The gypsy knew the boat would not dare land tonight. Instead of watching over the water, he stayed close to the campfire and smoked his tobacco.

He finished rolling another cigarette and looked over at the grazing horse. He did not trust it; there was something, something different about it and because it was different, he was afraid. He felt a great urge to be cruel and mistreat the creature but since the day he had knocked the horse half-senseless with his rifle, the animal had given him no cause; in fact, it had pulled the caravan at a pace no other horse had done before. Still, he did not like the animal; it made him fearful and put him on edge.

The gypsy moved closer to the fire and threw on some more wood. As he sat down, he found the horse was watching him and their eyes connected. Bracken's eyes glistened in the moonlight and in their depth the gypsy saw flames of swirling light. He discovered what it was he feared: the horse was not afraid of him.

The gypsy had been around horses all his life; they were in his blood. He knew about horses, or so he thought. You made them work all day, toiling and heaving under a heavy load. You whipped them and beat them to make them work harder and they complied because they were too scared and too stupid to step out of line and at the end of the day were grateful because you gave them a few oats or a feed of grass. They were dumb creatures – but this horse was different.

The gypsy continued to stare at Bracken, weighing him up. Then he stood up and threw his cigarette stub into the flames of the fire. It won't be long before I take it down to the knackers' yard, he thought. Next time the horse gives me trouble, I'll put a bullet in it.

He snarled at Bracken as he climbed up onto the caravan and went inside to sleep.

The following day was grey with cloud. The boat came in the night. She was a fifty-foot-long, twin-masted wooden fishing smack, ideal for smuggling. A small rowing boat attached to her stern floated in her wake. The smack glided stealthily into the secluded cove, her large forward mast already stowed; the smaller aft sail been lowered as she approached.

Two men were on the boat. One, an older man in his early fifties, wore a sea captain's peaked cap to cover his mop of curly grey hair. He was a big man in every way, broad and tall with a large belly to match his size. He was known simply as the 'Big

Man'. The second smuggler was younger, in his mid-twenties, and had the appearance and mannerisms of a rat. Unimaginatively, he answered to the name of 'Ratty'. Unfortunately, he did not possess the same level of intelligence as the beady-eyed rodent.

Ratty finished lowering the aft sail and began pulling in the rope attached to the rowing boat astern, bringing it alongside while the Big Man was up forward letting go the anchor.

The gypsy watched from the cliff top, leaning against one of the boulders. He could barely make out the two men on board but he knew them well enough. He had had dealings with the two smugglers in the past, as had many other gypsies. Straining his eyes in the dark, the gypsy watched as the two men loaded up the small wooden rowing boat, got on board and made for shore.

As the rowboat beached on the sandy shoreline, a flat-bedded wagon pulled by two horses with four men on board emerged from the cliff's overhanging shadows and made its way across the sand. At the same time the gypsy set off, making his way along a steep track that ran down the side of the cliff.

The smugglers met the four men and, with their help, started to unload the rowboat and carry its cargo over to the wagon. When the boat was empty the smugglers rowed back out to the smack and loaded the rowing boat once more before returning to shore. They made several trips and were on their last run when one of the men caught sight of the gypsy walking over the sand. Even in the dark the Big Man recognised him and told the others to carry on loading.

As the gypsy approached, he yelled to the Big Man, 'When you're done I need word.'

The Big Man was carrying a wooden crate in both hands. 'I'll be with you when I've loaded this,' he replied. The gypsy sat down on the sand and waited for him to finish.

With the last crate loaded, the four men jumped back on board the wagon and drove off, their horses straining as they pulled the heavy load back up the sandy beach. As they went, the Big Man nodded his head in the direction of the rowboat and spoke to Ratty. 'You go and wait for me in the boat. Shouldn't take long, this.'

The Big Man went over to the gypsy who stood up as he approached. Neither wasted time on formalities and the gypsy handed the photograph of Lady Elora to the smuggler.

'Not as pretty as the last one,' remarked the Big Man, glancing at the picture then stuffing it in his trouser back pocket.

'Never mind how pretty the bitch is,' the gypsy snarled. 'You know what to do?'

'Oh, I know what to do all right, matey,' said the Big Man. 'But before I does anything, I'd like to see the colour of your money.'

The gypsy pulled out one white fifty-pound note from his jacket.

'For that kind of money I'll make sure it's delivered,' said the smuggler. For a big man he moved surprisingly quickly as he snatched the money out of the gypsy's hand.

'If you know what good for you, you better. They'll be waiting when you land.'

The Big Man knew a threat when he heard one but chose not to reply. Instead he spat, aiming down between the gypsy's legs, turned and walked to the rowboat. He pushed the boat free of the beach, sat down alongside Ratty and picked up an oar. Together he and Ratty rowed the little boat back out to the smack.

The gypsy stood on the sand and watched until they got back on board and set sail before he made his way back up the cliff.

⚹ ⚹ ⚹

The gypsies were sitting on the harbour wall as the smugglers' boat sailed in. With the boat tied up alongside, two gypsies came on board and the Big Man handed over the photograph. The gypsies' stay on the boat was brief and they hardly said a word before they left; there was no need, they already knew what they had to do.

Chapter 31
BOUND AND DELIVERED

THEY CROSSED OVER the border into Romania and the poverty was evident. At one time, the gypsies would have had to traipse round the towns and villages, scouring the orphanages until they got lucky or in the end just settled for the nearest likeness they could find. It was not always easy and often took a lot of time and money to bribe the various officials and nuns who ran these places.

The crash of the American dollar made their life a lot easier.* The gypsies took full advantage; they did not have to go to orphanages any more to get what they wanted. In desperation, fathers and mothers parted with their children for a few coins if it meant they could survive for another day.

The gypsies had not travelled far before they found what they wanted, the first girl. A mother and her daughter were among

---

* For decades, Romania was a poor country. More than seventy per cent of the peasant population worked on the land. There was a shortage of draft animals to work the fields and a shortage of money, and technological backwardness meant even less machinery; without these, farmers could not increase their output. The situation was dire but to compound matters, Romania had one of the highest birth rates in the region; it could not grow enough nor had sufficient money to import food to support its people. Men, women and children were dying of malnutrition and disease. This already desperate country was battered in 1930 by the full force of the economic depression sweeping across the globe. The effect on the masses was ruinous and the people did everything and anything they could just to stay alive.

heaps of rotting garbage, scavenging for something – anything – to eat. The girl was fifteen years of age and her name was Cosmina. Although young and emaciated, her face was an exact likeness to the woman in the photograph.

One of the gypsies jumped down from the wagon, talked to Cosmina's mother and paid her. The woman clutched the coins they gave her tightly in one fist; the other hand held on to her daughter's skirt as she pleaded with the gypsies to look after her daughter and treat her well. They laughed at the woman as they tore her hand free and bundled Cosmina into the back of the caravan.

As the caravan moved away, Cosmina's mother looked down at her open palms. One held a few coins; the other was empty. She started to cry as she realised her belly would be full for the next few days but her heart would be empty forever.

Izolde was the name of the second girl. They found her alone, wandering the streets. She looked to be around sixteen – it was hard to tell because she was so filthy. Her long black hair caught their attention first. They asked her how old she was but she could not tell them because she did not know. She told them she had been living on the streets for a very long time. They got out the photograph and studied her face to ensure her likeness.

Izolde stretched out her neck to see what they held and saw the woman in the picture; she asked if it was her mother. 'Yes,' they said, 'would you like to see her?' She nodded and climbed into the caravan.

Having found what they came for, the gypsies turned round and headed out of Romania. Their next destination was a region in France where they had instructions to take the girls. Someone else would collect them and handle them from there; the gypsies had no doubt he would handle them all right.

The journey would take them a month and more and they had been warned the girls must remain hidden and concealed; no one must see them and the chattels were to be delivered in good condition. To the gypsies, 'good condition' meant that the girls should be treated like the rest of their animals; they gave them food and water, no more.

The girls, locked in the caravan as they travelled through the towns and villages, were let out just occasionally to bathe in a secluded river or stream. Even then the gypsies kept a close watch. If they spied anyone coming near they rushed down to the water and dragged the girls out, no matter what their state of undress, and bundled them back inside the caravan. The girls never dared scream or call for help; one of the gypsies had made it plain by drawing a dagger across his throat what would happen if they did.

If they were lucky, they were fed in the morning and again late in the evening when the gypsies stopped and made camp for the night. The girls would hear the key in the caravan door and one of the gypsies came in and gave them food and water. He stood over them watching, making sure they ate everything, his fist ready to strike if they did not; they had to look healthy when they were delivered.

Mid-morning on the thirty-eighth day, the caravan stopped and the girls heard the lock turn. This was not usual; they had already been fed. Izolde and Cosmina looked at each other, not knowing what to expect. Two gypsies walked through the caravan door; one held rope and silk neckerchiefs in his hands and the other carried two black hoods and a rusty old oil lamp.

The man holding the rope bound their hands tightly behind their backs then violently twisted the girls round, forcibly pulled down on their chins, squeezed their cheeks, parted their lips and stuffed a neckerchief into their open mouths. The other gypsy roughly pulled the black hoods down over their faces. There was a drawstring at the bottom of each hood; once the hoods were on, he pulled the drawstring tight around the girls' throats and made sure they were secure.

The gypsies pushed the bound, gagged and hooded girls down from the caravan and jostled them through the wood to a cave with bushes concealing the entrance. One gypsy held the branches apart and the other gypsy shoved the girls forward into the cave. Once inside they all stopped and waited as one of the gypsies lit the old oil lamp, then pushed the girls down a long, narrow tunnel. In many places, the ceiling was low and jagged rocks hung down. Herded down the tunnel, unable to see, the girls caught their heads on the outcrops of rock. Each time that happened, the gypsies thought it was hilarious and laughed loudly.

The gypsies herded the girls until they reached the back of the cave. Here the passage opened out into a small dome-like chamber. Ancient paintings of animals and handprints were scattered on the rocky walls. The gypsies paid no attention to the drawings; they forced the girls to sit and bring their knees up to their chests. They bound their ankles and brought up one end of the rope, pulled it forcefully between the girls' buttocks, looped the end round the rope binding their hands and tied it tight.

The gypsies left the two girls hooded, bound and unable to stand. As they made their way back along the tunnel, Cosmina and Izolde heard them laughing about how funny it was to see the girls hit their heads on the ceiling of the cave.

☒ ☒ ☒

Every evening the man left instructions with the stable hand to prepare his horse and have it saddled for him next morning. Straight after an early breakfast he rode out to the woods and, when deep inside, safely concealed amongst the trees and foliage, he halted his horse, dismounted and tied the animal securely to a thick branch. After that he trod stealthily through the undergrowth to a place close to the cave entrance where he hid in the bushes and trees.

Nothing had happened for days but this morning the caravan had made its rickety way along the woodland trail. Excited, the man watched as it stopped and its hooded cargo was unloaded and bundled inside the cave. As the branches concealing the cave entrance sprang back, the man got up slowly and retraced his steps.

He reached his horse, quickly untied it, mounted and rode back to his rambling chateau, his mind going over the details once more. The west wing of the chateau was a ruin. It was derelict, dangerous and isolated from the rest of the house. His cook and maid never went there. However, he would go there.

There were two rooms hidden in the rubble with stout doors and secure locks. The rooms had been prepared with the money he had received; they were identical and fitted for their intended purpose. These rooms were for the girls; no one would find them there.

Late in the evening he joined the maid and cook in the kitchen and slipped a sleeping potion into their cocoa. Before leaving, he double-checked their rooms to make sure they were sound asleep then silently made his way through the chateau and out to the stables. Under the cover of darkness, he picked up a lamp, saddled his horse and quietly led it out of the courtyard before mounting.

He rode through the woods to the mouth of the cave, drew back the branches and lit the lamp. Hurrying through the narrow tunnel, he reached the chamber. In the flickering lamplight he stopped to admire what he saw before him; it wasn't the prehistoric cave paintings!

He untied the rope around one of the girl's legs, hauled her to her feet and manhandled her back along the tunnel. He threw her over his horse and, with her bent over in front of him, rode back through the woods.

He rode hard to the old west wing, pulled the girl from the horse and bundled her through the crumbling corridors to the rooms. He unlocked one of the doors and pushed her inside. Hastily relocking the door behind him, he stuffed the key in his pocket and went back down the corridor. He had to hurry; he couldn't afford to take any chances. He had to get the other girl and bring her back before any of the staff began to wake up.

By the time he had locked the second girl in the other room his breathing was strained and he needed to rest. He sat down in the debris of the corridor and glanced, leering at the gas mask that was hanging on the wall between the two doors. His excitement rose. He didn't sit for long; he wanted to get started!

Wearing the mask, he entered the first room. Izolde sat on the floor shaking, terrified. He grabbed her roughly, pulled her up on her feet and dragged her to a bed against the wall. Fixed into the wall above the bed was an iron ring with a length of chain, metal collar and padlock attached to it. He placed the collar round Izolde's neck and snapped the lock closed.

A tin bath lay on the floor by the side of a white porcelain sink. He went to the sink, turned on the tap and filled a mug. He placed the mug on a small wooden table by the side of the bed. Izolde was facing away from him, trembling. He turned her round, yanked back the drawstring and removed the hood.

When her eyes regained focus she gazed upon the gas mask and panic overcame her. She couldn't scream; she began to faint. Her captor, seeing her state, slapped her hard and sent her sprawling across the bed. She looked up at him as he held up one finger in front of the mask to indicate that she should be quiet before drawing his hand menacingly across his neck, leaving her in no doubt that he would slit her throat if she was not. The man saw she understood. He grabbed hold of her again, pulled out the cloth from her mouth, rolled her onto her stomach and untied her hands. Then he stood and waited.

Izolde slowly turned onto her back and looked again upon the horror of the leather mask. The wearer pointed to the mug of water and, as she turned to drink, he left the room. He took the lamp with him and locked the door.

Izolde needed water desperately. She took hold of the mug and heard the rattle of the chain. As she drank, she felt the metal collar tighten around her throat.

In her hidden room Cosmina had managed to crawl to the bed and was sitting on the mattress. Her hooded face turned towards the door as she heard it open. She was not shaking or fearful; she sat rigid as if prepared. She had seen her mother sell her for a few coins. What more could anyone do to her?

She was to find out!

She heard water running, footsteps coming towards her and something being put down close by. She jerked back as she felt the tug at her neck and the savage blow at her head. Again, something tugged her neck; she stayed still. When the hood was removed and her eyes had cleared, she gazed with revulsion on the man who stared out at her from behind the small glass windows in his mask.

He took the metal collar from the bed and locked it round her neck. He hauled her to her feet, wrenched the neckerchief from her mouth, roughly turned her over and untied the ropes that were binding her hands. He held the mug of water out to her. She was dreadfully thirsty. As she reached out her hand, he dropped the mug and pushed her back on the mattress, forcing himself between her thighs. He especially liked something about this girl.

⚹ ⚹ ⚹

The days and weeks meant nothing: there was no routine, no regular comings or goings. The man wearing the mask came at all hours of the day and night to abuse them. When he brought food, he teased them with it and made them beg. Sometimes he put it just out of reach of their chains and left them for hours before coming back and watching them squirm, the collars cutting into their necks as they strained towards the plates. Sometimes he let them eat while he took them; at other times he didn't.

The girls, isolated, prisoners in their separate rooms, collared and chained, understand that if they hurt him in any way no one else would bring them food and they would starve. So as he abused them, they stayed still and complied.

After a time, things changed. The man came to Izolde but only with food; he never touched her. She was thankful but as time went on, she could still hear the sound of mumbled voices, the creaking of the bed and the rattling of Cosmina's chains through the wall. He was abusing Cosmina but not her; she began to wonder why.

As she grew rounder, whenever Izolde heard the man in Cosmina's room she went over to the dividing wall and pressed her ear against it to listen. The wall was too thick; all she could hear was muttering. Why did the man not take her? The thought began to pray on her mind and she grew jealous of Cosmina. She ached for him to touch her and longed to feel the glass and leather of his mask pressed up against her face once more.

Chapter 32
New Developments

One day a postman pedalled his bicycle up the drive to the manor. He carried an envelope addressed to the Peculiar Man; it had a foreign stamp and postmark.

The Peculiar Man opened the envelope over breakfast. It contained just one sheet of paper. The words, 'Start of new developments; all going to plan,' were written on it.

The Peculiar Man looked up and casually announced to his wife, seated across the table, that he fancied a change of air. She should get her maid to pack her things; they were going on a long vacation to the Highlands.

Lady Elora clapped her hands in delight. She loved the isolation of the Peculiar Man's Scottish lodge, away from the fuss of the servants. She found pleasure in the bleak, rugged landscape and remote glens of purple heather. She said she would see to matters immediately after breakfast. She hurriedly finished her smoked kippers and dashed away, leaving the Peculiar Man to enjoy his fruit compote.

Having eaten sufficient compote to ensure digestive regularity, the Peculiar Man retired to the study. He went to a small table covered with an assortment of silver-framed photographs and picked up one. He looked at the picture of himself and his young brother; the Peculiar Man was dressed in a black dinner suit and bow tie, his brother in army uniform. They had always been close; he wondered if it was because they had such a monster for a father. He held the picture for a while before putting it down, then he went to the bureau and started to write out a cheque.

Lady Elora was in her boudoir, fussing and fluttering round her maid, trying to decide what clothes to leave and what to pack in her trunk. She asked and answered her own questions. 'How many bonnets should I take? The weather is so changeable in the Highlands. I will need a hat for when it rains and a smaller hat for when it is windy so that my hair does not look untidy. And I must take my furs because it can get so cold. Oh dear, I have so much to think about. Why does my husband spring things on me so and make my life so difficult?'

Chapter 33
SILENCE IS GOLDEN

IT WAS THE last night that Cosmina and Izolde were to spend as prisoners chained in their hidden rooms. The man wearing the gas mask came in, tied their hands securely, gagged them and pulled down the black hoods. The padlocks snapped open and the metal collars were finally removed.

He forced Cosmina and Izolde back along the tunnel and dumped them on the floor in the painted chamber. They were confused and desperately frightened; they did not know what was going to happen to them. They could do nothing but wait in the cold and eerie silence of the cave. With every passing second, their fear grew.

It seemed like an eternity, their bodies cramped, aching unbearably. Then they heard a faint noise. The sound grew louder as it echoed in the painted chamber: it was the rumble of a wagon. Now they heard laughter, footsteps approaching down the tunnel. Someone cut the rope binding their ankles. They were dragged to their feet and lifted over shoulders; jagged rock tore into their backs as they were carried outside.

Inside the caravan, the hoods were removed and Cosmina and Izolde saw their captors' faces. They were the same gypsies who had taken them from Romania. It was almost twelve months since the girls had laid eyes on them.

The men left them tied up and locked the caravan door. They came back minutes later carrying two small bundles then the caravan set off to the harbour where the Big Man and Ratty waited.

$$\text{)( )( )(}$$

When the wooden fishing smack reached open water, the Big Man told Ratty to go inside, take off Cosmina and Izolde's gags and cut them free. Ratty looked up questioningly as if this was a stupid thing to do. Seeing the look on his face, the Big Man said, 'Do you think I'm daft, lad? Where do you think they are going to go in the middle of the English Channel? An' if they scream, who's flippin' well goin' to hear 'em, eh? Besides, they got things to take care of an' me and you are hardly equipped to do that.'

$$\text{)( )( )(}$$

The men wore flat caps and capes to keep out the October rain as they marched down the lane waving their blue-and-white 'Jarrow Crusade' banners.* The dark-haired gypsy waited and let the procession pass before turning the caravan into the lane and heading in the opposite direction. He drove on before eventually turning off and heading down the rutted, overgrown track.

He arrived at the jagged boulders at twilight.

The gypsy loathed the horse even more now and disliked going anywhere near it. He cursed the day he had bought Bracken.

---

* The men, about two hundred strong, were from the town of Jarrow in the north-east of England. They marched in a bid to gain respect and bring recognition to the plight of the numbers of unemployed throughout the country. They marched from their home town down to London, a distance of 300 miles, to hand in a petition to the British Prime Minister. The Prime Minister at the time, Stanley Baldwin, refused to see them, purposely ignoring their pleas for help.

Begrudgingly he released him from the shafts and tied him quickly to the back of the caravan. He would let the horse feed but he resented doing so. He would put up with the animal for the next few days because there was a lot of distance to cover but he would make sure he drove the beast hard along the way. And after he had made his delivery and bled the Peculiar Man dry, he would shoot it. The thought pleased him. It would not be a quick bullet in the head either; oh no, he'd make sure the damn creature suffered before it died. He imagined the horse writhing in agony, dying slowly, and the images pleased him.

He couldn't stand around all day. The light was fading fast and he wanted to go into the wood to lay some snares before it got too dark. He would be having company and extra food in the shape of a couple of rabbits wouldn't go amiss.

An hour or so later, the gypsy returned from setting his traps with a wild rabbit under his arm along with a few dry sticks to get the campfire going. He cooked and ate the rabbit then sprawled out in front of the fire, took out his tobacco tin and rolled a cigarette. He smoked it down to the tip then flicked the butt and watched it bounce off a large boulder towards the sea. As he looked, he caught sight of the wooden fishing boat sailing into the cove. It was a year since he had last stood on the beach and given the smugglers the photograph. The goods were almost in his hands.

He damped down the fire and set off along the steep, winding track down to the beach.

As the smack came to anchor, Ratty lowered the sails while the Big Man bound Cosmina and Izolde, tying their hands good and tight in front of them. He saw no need for hoods or gags; they were in the middle of nowhere in the middle of the night. With the girls secure, he brought the bundles up on deck as Ratty dropped the anchor and started to haul the rowboat alongside.

The gypsy stood on the beach, hearing the waves as they broke against the sandy shore. He watched the little rowboat come towards him, the oars dipping in and out of the black sea. Not long now and he would have his cargo; he had waited long enough.

The two smugglers gave a final heave on the oars and the rowboat surged through the water onto the beach. They got out and dragged the boat further up the shoreline. The Big Man helped the two girls out as Ratty climbed back on board to fetch the two bundles. He passed one to the Big Man before he stepped back onto the sand; as he did so, the baby wrapped inside began to cry.

Cosmina reached out with her bound arms for the child but Ratty pushed her away and shoved both her and Izolde ahead towards the gypsy who stood, arms folded across his chest.

The smugglers laid the babies on the sand in front of him. The gypsy looked at them, then at the two girls, then slowly at the smugglers. 'I think you have problem on your hands, yes?'

'What do you mean, problem? I hope this isn't one of your schemes to diddle us out of our money, Gypsy, cos be warned – there's two of us 'ere and we'll gut you if it is.'

As he spoke, a dagger appeared as if out of nowhere in the Big Man's hands and another in Ratty's. His arm was raised, the dagger held by the tip, ready to throw.

'I 'ave your money here as agreed so put down your knives,' the gypsy said. Then he pointed at the two girls. 'But looks like you brought more than I'm paying for. I have no room in the caravan for both of them.' Then, looking down at the babies, he added, 'And both of them as well.'

'Don't be daft,' sneered Ratty. 'The babies will die without a tit.'

'Doesn't know much, your boy, does he?' smirked the gypsy looking at the Big Man. He faced Ratty. 'Only need one pair of tits to feed babies; four tits is two too many for me. I have room only for one pair in caravan.'

'What are we goin' to do with 'em then?'

'Your problem,' said the gypsy. 'But I make it easy for you.' He nodded at Izolde. 'Cut that one free. I'll take her and both babies. She can help me carry them up the cliff. You do what you want with other one. Here's your money.' The gypsy threw the money on the sand.

Ratty picked it up and counted it. The Big Man kept his eye on the gypsy all the while. 'It's all 'ere,' Ratty said.

'Good. Now give me the money and go cut her free, like the gypsy said. We'll take the other one back in the boat with us.'

Ratty pushed Izolde forward without cutting her loose, gesturing at her to pick up a baby; she picked up her own child. The gypsy picked up the other and held it under one arm; with the other he took hold of Izolde's shoulder, clutching the material of her blouse tightly, and set off across the beach towards the cliff face.

Both girls had no idea what was happening but Cosmina saw her infant in the gypsy's arms and knew he was taking her baby away from her. Unlike her mother, she would not give up her child without a fight. Without warning, she ran forward and fell into the back of the gypsy's legs, tripping him.

The gypsy got up, the baby still held under his arm. Cosmina was on her knees in front of him, her tied hands held out as if in prayer, begging him not to take her child. 'I have no time for this,' said the gypsy, suddenly bringing up his knee sharply and smashing it into her face, knocking her out cold. He turned back to Izolde, grabbed hold of her again and dragged her over the sand to the cliff and on up the steep, winding track back up to the caravan.

The two smugglers were all for leaving Cosmina on the beach. They had their money, what did they care? Only the thought that the authorities, the police, customs and excise could discover the girl and their investigations might lead to them worried them.

They picked up Cosmina and hauled her back into the rowboat.

Bracken's ears pricked up as he caught the odour of the gypsy on the sea breeze and heard his footsteps. He detected new scents too, that of Izolde together with young animals, the babies.

The gypsy and the girl came up from the cliff to the side of the caravan. The gypsy spoke in Romanian for the first time. 'Put the baby on the ground and get up there.'

Izolde did as she was told; she put the infant down on the grass and climbed on board the caravan. The gypsy jumped up after her and motioned with his head for her to open the door and go inside. He followed her in and shoved her onto the bed at the back.

The gypsy put the baby down on the bed and took out his knife. Seeing the blade, the colour drained from Izolde's face. The gypsy grabbed her; she could not help but scream out loud. The scream pierced Bracken's ears and he curled his lips and bared his teeth.

The gypsy cuffed Izolde, silencing her. 'If I want to kill you, do you think I would shove the blade in you here and mess up my home with your blood? Do you?' With one quick slash, he cut the ropes round her wrists. 'Now get on and do what you have to with the brat and get it fed.'

He left Izolde, went outside and returned with the other baby. He placed the infant on the bed and said, 'Feed this brat also.'

The gypsy opened a cupboard, rummaged inside and brought out a bottle of milk. He started to drink from the bottle as he watched Izolde feed the babies. When she had finished he opened the cupboard again, took out some bread, gave it to her and filled a tin cup with milk. While she ate, he went outside to the back of the caravan, removed the little pin and caught the door of the secret compartment as it dropped open. The gypsy had lined the hiding place with thick padding; anyone locked inside could scream as loud as they wanted but nobody would hear.

He went back inside the caravan. Izolde sat on the bed between the two sleeping infants, picking at the crust of bread, putting little pieces into her mouth. As she ate, the gypsy gathered up the infants, went back outside and placed them in the soundproofed secret compartment. He pushed them to the back as far as they would go.

When he returned Izolde was still sitting where he had left her, picking at the bread. 'You,' he said, pushing the tin cup towards her, 'finish milk and come here. Bring your bread.'

Izolde picked up the cup and drank until it was empty. Afraid, clutching the bread to her breast, she moved nervously towards the gypsy. His hand shot out and he grabbed hold of Izolde's long black hair and dragged her down off the caravan to the back of the wagon.

'Get in,' he ordered.

Izolde looked at the space where the babies lay; it was cramped and too small. She would never be able to breathe in there. Terrified, she pleaded, 'I don't want to go in there. Please don't make me go in there. It is too small for me, I'm afraid of small spaces. I'll be good, I'll do anything. I'll do anything for you, anything you want but please, please don't make me go in there.'

The gypsy clenched his fist, drew back his arm and punched her hard in the stomach. As Izolde doubled up under the blow, he pushed her head back, grabbed hold of her ankles and rolled her into the compartment. Then he slammed the door shut, fitted the locking pin and said, 'I don't want to be up all night keeping my eye on you. There are long days of travelling ahead. I need to get a good night's sleep.' Then he fell silent thinking, why am I talking, wasting my breath? She won't be able to hear me anyway. And he laughed.

In the cramped, padded compartment, Izolde could not hear the gypsy and the gypsy could not hear Izolde if she muttered, talked, shouted or screamed for dear life – but Bracken could. His funnel-shaped ears had evolved to capture the slightest sound and were capable of detecting far higher and lower frequency noise than any human ear. He heard Izolde gulping for air, her hand slapping against the side of the secret door, trying to get free. He sensed her fear. Bracken heard her breathing become shallow and slow down as she accepted that she was going to die. Then he heard her soft, pitiful whimpers.

Bracken heard her every sound and sensed her every emotion.

✗ ✗ ✗

Cosmina came round as the smugglers upped anchor. She was dazed and confused but consciousness came quickly: her baby, where was her baby? She tried to stand but, groggy and with the swaying of the boat as it tossed and rolled in the waves, she lost her footing and fell back down. She tried again and managed to stay on her feet, caught sight of the big smuggler and staggered like an inebriated sot, shouting at him, screeching, 'Where is my baby? Where is my baby? What have you done with him? Give me my baby, give me my baby.'

She fell upon him, beating him with her fists. The Big Man caught hold of her arms and shouted for Ratty as she tried to claw at his eyes. Ratty came running, took hold of Cosmina from behind and threw her down on the deck. Demented, she sprang up and went for both of them but Ratty was fast; he hit her hard and knocked the wind out of her. She collapsed onto the deck, heaving.

'You'll stay put, do you hear? If you know what's good for you, you'll bloody well stay put,' Ratty snarled, eyes blazing, looking down at her.

Cosmina, struggling to catch her breath, heard his words but did not understand; the men did not understand her either. They spoke in different tongues. She lay doubled up on the deck, stricken with grief, realising the full hopelessness of her plight. She began to wail, knowing that her baby boy was lost forever.

Cosmina could not be calmed. After a while the Big Man went over to her to try to stop her caterwauling but she was beyond despair, beyond reasoning with. He and Ratty stayed away from her after that, hoping she would eventually quieten down; she did not. If anything, her bawling got worse as they sailed back across the channel. It was getting on the two smugglers' nerves.

'For God's sake, I can't stand it any more. Ratty, go an' sort her out, I can't put up with her bloody shrieking any longer.' The Big Man watched from the wheel of the boat as Ratty scurried across the deck, whipped out his knife and, in the blink of an eye, slit her throat.

The Big Man was not expecting that. He'd expected Ratty to gag her, knock her out or something, but not that. He should have known better but that was Ratty for you. 'Suppose that was one way to shut her up,' the Big Man said, leaving the wheel.

Ratty smiled as the two of them lifted Cosmina and threw her overboard. 'Silence is golden,' the Big Man said as a requiem, as her body hit the sea.

Chapter 34
DON'T COUNT YOUR CHICKENS

HE WOKE EARLY; he had slept well, very well. He turned over on his back, his eyes open, but he did not see anything except what was in his mind. Everything had gone well so far, better than expected. He had made sure they used two girls, just in case one of the babies or the mothers died or had a girl child; as it was, all had lived and both children were boys. He would deliver the babies and persuade the Peculiar Man to take both – at an extra cost, of course.

He could hear himself now: 'Just imagine what a great man your friends will think you, and how happy you'll make your wife's mother and father. How powerful they will think your loins that you can produce two children, twins, in one go.' The gypsy knew that an excuse for a man such as the Peculiar Man would not be able to say no. The Peculiar Man would pay for both brats all right, he was sure of that; but if he did not, what did he care? He would kill one of the babies and dump its body. Besides, if the Peculiar Man thought he could get away with paying a one-off miserly pittance then he was as much a brainless fool as he was a seedless eunuch. Once the Peculiar Man announced to the world he was a father, the gypsy would blackmail him for the rest of his life.

The gypsy continued to laze on his bed and imagine what he

would buy with the Peculiar Man's money. A new horse first – but only after he had had his fun and made the one outside suffer.

Happy as he was lying there daydreaming, the gypsy had things to do. He got up, took hold of his rifle and went back into the woods to check on his traps; a rabbit or two should have wriggled itself to death by now. Later he would come back, get a fire going and cook breakfast. Then he'd let the bitch and the babies out. She could feed them and it would give her some exercise before he sealed her up again and went on his way.

It would take him eight or nine days to reach the highlands of Scotland, ten at the most. Then he would be rich, rich for the rest of his life, and he intended to live a long life.

Izolde was mercifully asleep. One of the babies started to cry and set the other off howling. Izolde woke, disorientated, confused; it was pitch black inside the compartment. Where were the babies? She couldn't see the babies. They were crying for food. She needed to feed them.

She felt round and found one but there was not enough space to pull it to her breast. She struggled, jiggling her body into a position so the baby could feed. It was too cramped, too confined, she couldn't turn to feed the baby. The babies were bawling...

She felt pain in her stomach, a desperate need to pee. Panic rose inside her and she lost control. She screamed and screamed and screamed.

Bracken sensed Izolde's fear. His sensitive ears heard all. He reared up, powerful hind legs thrusting him into the air. The tether around his neck jerked tight and the caravan lifted. Mighty muscles bulging, he rose higher still. He came down, the caravan crashing, rocking from side to side as it hit the ground. Up again he reared, raising the caravan off its wheels, then it came thumping back down. He rose higher still, the caravan landing, bouncing, shaking, rattling from side to side, Izolde's frantic screams driving him on. Again he reared, muscles pumping like huge pistons, neck straining, tether stretched tight; then it snapped.

All four wheels of the caravan remained firmly on the ground.

Bracken could hear Izolde's screams and the babies' howls. He could sense their desperation, their fear. The tether was broken but he was now free to move. He stepped to the centre, at the back of the caravan, and kicked the underside of the secret door. With all the crashing, shaking, rocking and rolling, the locking pin was almost out; another kick and it was free. The secret door dropped open and Izolde tumbled out onto the ground.

Her hair and her clothes were soaking with sweat and piss. Her eyes were wild; she retched as she lay, throwing up on the grass. Breathing deeply, her eyes cleared as if the dread had left her together with the vomit, but only for a split second. Her eyes clouded over with renewed terror as the gypsy, rifle waving in the air, came running out of the woods towards them.

Bracken heard the gypsy coming long before Izolde saw him and was already racing across the ground, hurtling towards him. The gypsy had no chance to get out of the way of the charging horse. The full might of Bracken hit him and hurled him backwards; the gypsy crashed into the boulders and smashed his head against the rocks. Blood dripping from his head, pinned against the wall of rock, the man couldn't escape. Bracken leapt, his forelegs rearing up and up, his neck stretching, and his hooves caught the gypsy's hand and sent the rifle flying.

An explosion split the air. It was all too much for the noble horse who succumbed to his evolutionary reaction to survive. Bracken turned from the gypsy; he could no longer suppress his natural urge to take flight. But as he ran, something struck him. He did not stop; instinct propelled him forward, his hooves pounding the earth, speeding away over the ground.

As Bracken flew past the caravan, Izolde saw her chance. She jumped quickly onto the secret compartment's overhanging door and leapt for her life. She landed hard, thumping onto Bracken's back. She caught hold of his streaming black mane, desperately clinging on. The horse moved like the wind, his actions governed by thousands of years of evolved response to danger.

Bracken galloped on and on until he was far from peril and his mighty lungs could no longer supply the oxygen to feed his powerful muscles. He slowed to a trot and the girl on his back knew that for the moment she was safe; they had left the gypsy far behind.

The rifle went spinning, spinning through the air, tumbling round until it fell, sliding and clattering between the boulders. The trigger caught on a jagged piece of rock and the gun went off. The gypsy felt the full force of the stray bullet as it ripped into his guts. Blood streaming from his forehead, he looked down at his belly and saw his innards oozing out.

He slid slowly down the cold stone as the unbearable pain hit him and writhed on the ground, the screams of his slow, agonising death echoing round the standing boulders.

Chapter 35
POLITIA A VENI

BRACKEN WAS HEADING along the coast road, Izolde still on his back. Although she had escaped, she was weary and fearful for her own and Cosmina's babies. What was she to do? She could not leave the babies with that monster. She needed to find help.

Coming to a bend, through the trees at the side of the road, she caught sight of cottages dotted around a small harbour down below. A few fishing boats lay tied up alongside the quay. Round the bend, she saw a lane off to the right leading towards the harbour. She pulled Bracken's mane, turned the horse to head down the road and made for the fishing port.

The village appeared deserted except for two fishermen who were standing next to the harbour wall, mending their nets. At the sound of Bracken's hooves they stopped and looked over at the girl on the horse that was coming down the lane. From the state of her they sensed that something was wrong. Both men left their nets and ran over to help.

The first fisherman to reach them grabbed Bracken's halter, saying softly, 'Easy boy, easy there. Whoa, there's a good lad.' He managed to stop the horse and, while he held him steady, the other fisherman gently took hold of Izolde and eased her off Bracken's back.

Izolde tried to speak to them, to make them understand that

she needed help, the babies needed help, but the men looked confused; they did not understand her foreign tongue. Then Frank, the fisherman who had helped her down off Bracken and was still supporting her, said, 'Danny, I think we need to get her over to the police station.'

Izolde recognised the word 'police'. '*Politia, politia! Da, da, politia,*' she said anxiously. '*Politia, da.*'

'By the sounds of it I think you're right, Frank. Come on, let's get her down there.'

Danny took Izolde to the constable on the desk and started to tell him what little he could. When Izolde saw the police officer's uniform, she knew this was the man to help her. She reached over the desk and clasped the constable's hand, imploring, '*Politia a veni. Politia a veni da.*'*

'I think she wants you to go with her,' said Danny, looking at the constable.

Izolde removed her hand from the police officer as he came round the desk but, as soon as he was beside them, she clasped hold of him again, tugging him towards the door, waving with her other arm for the fishermen. '*A veni, a veni. Da, da,*' she shouted.

'Wait,' said the policeman, pulling back. 'I don't get a good feeling about this at all, not if she wants us all to go. Danny, Frank, just stay here with her for a second while I have a word with the sarge.'

The constable went back behind the desk and poked his head round the sergeant's door. 'Sarge, do you mind coming out and having a look at this? You might want to get involved.'

The sergeant came out and took one look at the fearful state of the girl. She had desperation written all over her but, before he got a chance to say anything, Izolde opened the door and rushed outside. All four men followed and looked as she stood in the lane and pointed up towards the cliff top shouting, '*A veni, a veni. Da.*'

* 'Policeman come. Policeman come, yes.'

186

The sergeant looked up at the cliff top then told the constable to nip back inside, get the keys off his desk and bring the car round. As they waited in the lane, Izolde kept pointing and pleading, '*A veni, a veni.*' Only when the black police car appeared and the sergeant put her in the front passenger seat did she begin to calm down as she pointed out to the constable where to go.

They found the babies asleep in the secret compartment of the gypsy's caravan. The body of the dark-haired gypsy was slumped at the bottom of a boulder. Looking at the gypsy, the sergeant was thankful that none of them had encountered the man when he was alive. Even lying there with his entrails hanging out he looked a bad sort. Nevertheless, the sergeant could not help but wonder if the gypsy was evil enough to die like this; a bullet in the guts meant only one thing, a slow, agonising death.

In their haste and with everything that was happening, everybody forgot about Bracken who was left standing outside the police station. After a while, he trotted back down the lane, past the hanging fishing nets and over to the cottages. There he leaned his neck over a short wooden fence that surrounded the front garden of one of the white-walled cottages and started nibbling the lawn. Sometime later, he trotted out of the village.

Up on the cliff top there was not much more anyone could do. The sergeant told the constable to drive Izolde, the babies, Frank and Danny back to the village, then to get on the phone, inform headquarters what had taken place and get them to send an investigation team round along with someone to collect the body. 'Once you've done that, take the babies and girl to the cottage hospital. Have a doctor check them out. I'll wait here until you get back.'

The constable dropped the fishermen off, parked outside the police station, went inside with Izolde and made the phone call. Satisfied that HQ was fully briefed, he drove to the hospital with Izolde and the babies.

The constable remained in the waiting room as Izolde and the babies went with a nurse into a screened cubicle. Shortly afterwards a doctor approached and told him that Izolde and the babies were undernourished and showed symptoms of dehydration. He wanted to admit them for three or four days to build them up, just to be on the safe side. After that he saw no reason why they couldn't be discharged.

The constable thanked the doctor and said he would be back later to find out how the girl was and to ask her some questions. Before he left he said, 'By the way, doctor, have you any idea what nationality she is? It would save a bit of time. I'll need to get an interpreter and it would help if I knew what language she spoke.'

'I can't really say,' the doctor replied. 'At a guess, something Eastern European.'

〤 〤 〤

Several miles down the coast, Cosmina's body was washed ashore on the incoming tide. Jim Cosgrove was a fit young man in the habit of rising early and going for a run along the beach with his two black-and-white sheepdogs, Tessa and Kelly. The two dogs found Cosmina's body lying head down in the sand. Their barking brought Jim over and, as he reached her, she raised her sand-covered face and looked at him through half-open eyes.

〤 〤 〤

While Izolde was in hospital, quite a few officials came to ask her questions and get information. On the third day, however, late in the evening when all was quiet on the ward, a man wearing a red felt hat sat down by her bed. He talked quietly to her; his accent was English, his Romanian poor.

After he left, Izolde drew her knees up and pulled the bedcovers over her head. She was very frightened. She was in a strange country, she did not speak the language and she had herself and two babies to look after and no money. What was she to do?

Early on the fourth day Izolde dressed quietly and walked out of the ward, holding the warmly wrapped babies in her arms. At the end of the lane that led to the cottage hospital, she saw the man in the red felt hat. He was sitting in a gaily decorated horse-drawn caravan. Beside him was a young woman; she held a baby girl of about three months of age to her breast.

Izolde walked to the caravan and held up Cosmina's baby. The gypsy took it, passed it to the woman next to him and handed over money to Izolde. Standing in the lane with the money and her own baby safe in her arms, Izolde watched as the gypsy doffed his red felt hat to her, flicked the reins and the caravan moved off.

The gypsy with the red felt hat had no time to waste. He had to get up to Scotland and he had a long way to go.

Chapter 36
BACK HOME

THE PECULIAR MAN'S estate manager was the first to spot Bracken. He was out on his rounds, about to turn his horse-drawn buggy into the lane on his way up to check on what had been the Bradshaw's farmhouse and outbuildings, when he saw the horse in the field.

He recognised Bracken almost immediately. The farmhouse had remained empty since Ned's death, so how on earth the horse had got into the field the manager did not know. He could only assume that Bracken had jumped the hedge or the white gate, because from where he sat the gate looked firmly closed and there was no other way in.

The manager pulled in to the side of the lane, sat back in the padded seat of his two-wheeled carriage and watched the horse. Bracken cropped the grass, lifted his head and cantered up to the old bathtub where he drank, splashing water over the sides of the tub. He shook his head busily then cantered away over the field.

The estate manager would never profess to have Ned Bradshaw's experience and knowledge of animals but it was abundantly clear even to him that he was looking at one very happy horse.

After watching Bracken for a while the estate manager, a smile upon his face, moved up to the top of the farm. On his way he stopped at the white gate. Jumping down from his buggy, he shouted and whistled to Bracken. With his chest out and head held high, Bracken cantered proudly over to the man. The estate manager stroked Bracken's head and nose, and gently pulled his ears and patted his neck. Bracken reached his big head forward and nibbled the manager's ear. The estate manager's smile grew even wider.

The estate manager was a busy man though and, much as he would have liked to, he could not stand stroking Bracken all day; he had work to do. He gave Bracken's neck a final pat then got back on his buggy and drove up to the white-walled farmhouse. He went round the building and the barn and checked the structure, roofs and the guttering. After completing his inspection he set off to see Christine; he had heard she was living with Ned's mother in a cottage nearer to town.

As he drove out of the farm he looked back at Bracken. The horse was grazing at the bottom of the field; rabbits were nibbling grass by his feet.

The estate manager arrived at the small cottage opposite the local pub, the Swan and Cemetery. He had spent many of his younger days in there with Ned and Nathanial. Both were good men, he thought; it was a pity the world didn't have more like them. After he'd had a quick word with Christine, he'd nip over and treat himself to a pint in their memory, he decided.

The manager knocked on the cottage door. Christine answered, invited him through to the small, comfortable front parlour and begged him to sit down and make himself comfortable. The manager waited for Christine to sit before he told her about seeing Bracken up at the farm and asked what she wanted him to do with the horse.

Christine was surprised at the news and did not know what to do. She believed someone had bought Bracken and he did not belong to her any more. Seeing her at something of a loss, the estate manager suggested she could leave Bracken in the field for now. No harm would come to him there and, if no one came to claim him in a few days, perhaps her mother-in-law could have a word at the dairy and see if they wanted Bracken. It was common knowledge that the dairy was always on the lookout for good horses.

Christine thanked the manager. As she saw him out, she asked if he would let her know if anyone came for the horse. If not, she would get Ned's mother to speak to the dairy.

He assured her he would and, after saying his goodbyes, he crossed over the road to the Swan and Cemetery.

Several days later, a man from the dairy went up to the farm and collected Bracken. Later that day the same man went to the cottage to give Christine some money for the horse but she would not accept it. The man was in a bit of a pickle; he tried to insist that she take the money but Christine would have none of it. Bracken had been sold and she was not his legal owner any more. How could she possibly take money for him? She closed the door politely on the man.

Chapter 37
WHISTLE WHILE YOU WORK

BRACKEN WAS LED round the back of the main building at Wilkinson's Dairy to the stables. They consisted of two ramshackle wooden buildings that faced each other, separated by a narrow path. Each block had eight stalls and each stall had a rusty number nailed to the door. Bracken was put in stall number eight.

The next morning was very windy. A man came at 4.00a.m. He was wearing a long white, button-through coat, blue trousers, a pair of black boots and a blue peaked cap. As he went to the stall door, the wind blew the cap off his bald head and he had to run and chase it as it rolled across the yard. When he caught it, he pressed it firmly back down on his head, holding on to it as he walked back to the stall and unbolted the door.

Bracken moved eagerly forward but the man caught hold of his halter and held him back. 'Whoa there, boy, whoa. You're keen! It's nice to see,' he said and patted Bracken, adding in a more sombre tone, 'I wonder if you'll be so eager in another year or two?'

The man brought Bracken out of the stall and led him into a rectangular yard where a number of four-wheeled milk carts were lined up in a row. He backed Bracken up and hitched him to one of the carts, jumped on board and drove round to the concrete loading bay. When the cart was fully loaded the man set off.

Bracken pulled the cart across the yard, out through the painted gates and onto the cobbled streets.

The milkman had a firm but gentle way with the reins and as they went along he talked continually to Bracken. Sometimes he had to shout to make himself heard over the noise of the blustery wind. Bracken's sensitive ears picked up everything, especially the calm, kind tone of the man's voice.

Responding to a slight flick of the reins, Bracken turned into one street and then into another and another. All of them looked the same. Some streets funnelled the wind, making it howl across the cobbles, and Bracken pinned back his ears and put his head down as he pulled the float. Other streets offered shelter, the terraced houses acting as barriers against the wind, and here the milkman stopped talking, put his lips together and whistled a tuneless whistle.

Bracken pulled the milk float effortlessly through the streets but in one the wind was exceptionally gusty and, as he moved along with his head down, he felt something brush against his foreleg. It was a double page from a newspaper that had blown from across the other side of the street. As he walked on, Bracken raised his hoof higher to rid himself of the irritating paper. The wind picked up as he did so and the page flapped open to reveal a photograph of two almost identical-looking men. A woman stood between them cradling a baby. The accompanying headline read: *Lady Elora and Her Husband Celebrate Birth of Baby Boy*. The next line read: *Younger brother arrives from France to celebrate with happy couple…*

Bracken raised his hoof higher and the paper blew away. He turned into yet another dreary street. The street was sheltered and, in the absence of the wind, the milkman broke into another tuneless whistle.

After that day Bracken never again saw the milkman with the tuneless whistle. At 4.00a.m. the following morning a different man came and opened the door to his stall. He wore the same coloured uniform, blue peaked cap, long white coat and blue trousers but he did not whistle and never spoke a word; not to Bracken, anyway. The man was sullen, downcast, as if he had nothing left to live for. It was as if life itself had been sucked from him. His name was Mr Bob Brown.

Chapter 38
A Child is Forever

THE GYPSY WITH the red felt hat arrived. Lady Elora was excited; at last, she had a baby. The Peculiar Man had mixed emotions; he was relieved that he finally had an heir but he was annoyed that the gypsy was late. He should have been there days ago and the Peculiar Man was not accustomed to waiting. Once he got his wife out of the room, he would have strong words with the gypsy, he was in no doubt about that.

Lady Elora held the baby and tickled him under his chin. 'We'll call you Jonathon, won't we?' she said, looking down at the swaddled baby. 'Yes, you're my little Jonnykins, aren't you? My little Jonnykins, yes, you are,' she cooed.

The men stood silently for a moment watching her fawn over little Jonnykins, before the Peculiar Man addressed his wife. 'I think the baby looks hungry, my dear. Do you not think it would be a good idea to take him to the wet nurse for a feed?'

'Oh my, yes,' replied his wife. 'We can't have my little Jonnykins getting hungry, can we?'

The Peculiar Man waited until the door closed behind her then took up matters with the gypsy. 'Now, look here,' said the Peculiar Man. 'I want to talk to you about your fee.'

'Good, so do I,' the gypsy said quietly. The Peculiar Man

completely ignored him as if the man had not moved his lips. Undaunted, he continued, 'We agreed a specific time for the delivery of the child and you did not keep to our arrangement. I paid your accomplice up front as agreed but as you have not met our terms, so I demand money back in recompense.'

The Peculiar Man put both hands on his hips and stuck out his chin in a rather supercilious pose to show that he would brook no argument. The gypsy looked at him and slowly shook his head. He put his hand in his trouser pocket and pulled out a crumpled piece of paper. He handed it to the Peculiar Man. There was a number written on it.

'What's this supposed to be?' asked the Peculiar Man angrily, staring down at the figure on the paper.

'It's the amount of money you will pay me every month,' said the gypsy quietly. 'Make sure you have it. I'd hate for the press to find out who Jonnykins' real mother and father are, wouldn't you? Have the money ready at the beginning of each month. Someone will be round to collect it.'

Once outside, the gypsy donned his red felt hat and walked away from the lodge to the sound of a baby crying.

THE STORY: PART THREE

Chapter 39
NO LAST WORDS

THE DEPRESSION BIT deeper every day.

Millions unemployed, millions in poverty, millions undernourished and no one came to help.

The rich and powerful went about their lives seemingly without care for those to whom they owed so much.

Mr Bob Brown had been coming to the stable every day, six days a week, for the past two years and in all that time he had never once spoken a word or shown Bracken any tenderness.

On the first morning when Bob drew back the bolt to open stall number eight, if he could only have raised enough enthusiasm to open his eyes properly he would have seen a fine animal, a proud, noble animal, muscles rippling, coat gleaming, ready and eager to meet the challenges of the day. But Bob could not raise enough enthusiasm.

If Mr Brown could have mustered a tiny bit of enthusiasm for life, opened his eyes a fraction and seen what stood before him now, he would have been truly ashamed. With its head hung low, its ears folded back, here was a horse with a dull dry coat, matted mane and tail, an animal virtually as devoid of life as Bob himself; a truly sorrowful sight.

But Bob didn't want to open his eyes; he did not want to see the reality before him. Bob had seen reality once upon a time and never wanted to see it again.

But this morning it was there before him.

He had found it as, half asleep, he dressed in his milkman's uniform and made his way from his lonely bedroom across the little square landing. He tripped, accidentally knocking against the picture that hung at the top of the stairs. Jarred free from years of dirt and dust, the picture swung backwards and a letter slipped from behind it, her letter. It fell to the floor.

As soon as Bob saw it, he knew what it was. A cold sweat broke out on his face and he rushed out of the house and down to the dairy, trying to forget, trying to find safety in routine. But his day was only going to get worse.

✗ ✗ ✗

Joe Wilson tried to smarten up before he left the boarding house. He pinned his campaign medals above his breast pocket but somehow they looked out of place; they had been awarded for victory and valour but what sort of victory was this?

He stood mute, looking down into the grave. He did not feel the pains of hunger in his belly today. Neither did he feel the pelting rain or the soaked, ragged jacket that was hanging loose about his emaciated frame.

As his wife's coffin descended into the grave, he raised his eyes and caught sight of the new tombstone. It had cost his last penny. Silently he mouthed the inscription: 'Here lies Mary Wilson, aged 38yrs, beloved wife of Joe, now at rest with her children.' Underneath were their names: 'Joseph, died aged 10yrs 2mths; Agnes, died 2yrs 4mths; Maud, died aged 1yr 2mths'.

Three times Joe had stood by this graveside and three times he had said a final goodbye.

When the funeral service was over, and after the few that came to pay their respects had departed, Joe remained alone, staring down mesmerized as the rain hit the sodden earth, forming pockmarked craters in the fresh dirt that covered his family.

He had served his country, done his duty … but for what?

Hands in pockets, he stood by the grave until late afternoon when the downpour eased to a drizzle. Then, looking at the words on the gravestone once more, he slowly turned and wandered back to the boarding house.

Earlier that morning the landlady had no sooner heard his footsteps coming down the stairs and the front door close behind him than she was up in his room packing his things. She stuffed what little he had into a brown paper bag and placed it in the hallway at the bottom of the stairs. She was waiting for him now, perched by the 'No Vacancies' sign hanging in the window.

She caught sight of him as he turned the corner and came down the cobbled street. She waited until he was outside the house, then stamped into the hallway, snatched up the paper bag, opened the door and threw it at him, shouting, 'Don't pay yer rent, yer don't get a room. I runs a business I does, not a bleeding charity shop. Now off with yer, yer good for nothing lowlife.'

She went back inside, slamming the door behind her. Joe stooped and picked up his things off the cobbles and placed them back in the bag. He put the bag under his arm and walked on without saying a word.

A solitary figure, not knowing or caring where he went, Joe walked the streets throughout the night. Eventually he could walk no further; he felt dizzy and light-headed and had to stop. He clung to a lamp-post for support. The lamp was one of those new electric arc lights; he kept hold of it, afraid to let go in case he fell.

Joe stood in the beam of white luminescence and looked up at the candescent globe and the wrought-iron pole from which it hung; he liked the old gaslights better, their glow was softer.

He noticed the dawn breaking in the sky. He thought the electric companies would switch off the street lights soon.

He drew his old service revolver from his pocket. It was a memento from the trenches. Joe looked down at the loaded gun that was resting in the palm of his hand.

✕ ✕ ✕

Bob opened stall number eight and led Bracken out into the yard. When Bracken was standing between the shafts, he placed the harness on the horse's back and attached the traces. With the straps and buckles tied and tight, Mr Brown climbed on board and drove the wagon round to the loading ramp at the front of the dairy.

Bracken pulled the laden cart around the cobbled streets as Bob jumped on and off delivering milk, placing the bottles neatly to one side on the doorsteps of the terraced houses. He found some kind of peace in the routine but things were about to change.

In Darcy Street, towards the end of the delivery, Bracken's nostrils began to twitch. A quiver ran down his flanks; he could smell blood. Below the lamp-post, at the far end of the street, a man's body lay on the pavement. There were medals pinned to his worn suit jacket. A service revolver lay by his outstretched arm and there was a gaping hole the size of a small child's fist in the middle of his head.

The milk float pulled alongside and Mr Bob Brown stared down wide-eyed. He did not want to see this, he most certainly did not. Shaking uncontrollably, he looked down and gawped at his old friend, Joe Wilson.

Excruciating pain burst inside Bob's head. He squeezed his eyes closed, covering them with his hands, pressing hard, fighting the pain, fighting to hold back the memories, fighting to hold back his sobbing, but the teardrops ran through his fingers.

He had tried so hard, broken all connections and shunned them all. Why, why could they not leave him alone? Why could they not stay away, stay away from him, stay away so he could forget? His questions went unanswered. Teetering on the edge for so long, seeing Joe, opened the chasm and the painful memories came flooding back.

He pushed his eyeballs further into their sockets, his face screwed agonisingly tight as he tried to stop the final abomination materialising inside his head, but to no avail. He saw everything, saw them all pressed tight against the wall of the trench, up to their knees in mud. He heard the deafening noise, the exploding artillery shells, saw the blinding white light, shrapnel, bullets whizzing past. Saw the dismembered dead and dying men all around, the gas, the rats, the lice, the mindless suffering, misery and horror.

He saw his beloved wife Martha, her body dangling from a noose. He saw the letter drop from behind the picture this very morning.

Bob hunched in the milk float, a quivering, sobbing wreck.

Bracken moved on past Joe Wilson's eternally mute body and pulled the wagon back to the dairy.

By the time they reached Wilkinson's Bob had stopped crying. He went about his work mechanically, unhitched Bracken, led him back into the stall and turned to leave. Then he hesitated and looked at Bracken as if…

Bob's mouth moved a fraction but without uttering a word he closed and bolted the stable door, turned and went home.

He shut the door of his empty house. The only greeting was the sound from the parlour of the ticking of the fireside clock. Terrified, he looked at the picture that was hanging aslant on the wall; then he looked at the stairs, each step a mountain he knew he must climb. Climb he did, utterly weary, drenched in sweat, until he collapsed at the top.

With shaking hands, he reached out and grasped her letter.

He forced himself to read.

Martha's letter opened his eyes.

He slumped on the stairs, head in his hands, seeing everything clearly. Memories of the suffering, the pain, the injustice, filled the hours. When would it all end…?

Only when he relived it all.

Chapter 40
THE BEGINNING

HE WAS NOTHING but a fresh-faced youth in a man's body, proud and eager to fight for king and country in the great cause. He did not know or understand what the great cause was, mind you, or even what the war was all about, but he knew it must be great. After all, the politicians and grand men who spoke in public and wrote in the newspapers said so.

It was Saturday night. Bob had arranged to meet his girl before seeing his best mate Joe Wilson down in the Swan and Cemetery. Now he was on his way up to the manor house to wait in the gardens for Martha. Martha worked in service for the Peculiar Man. She'd already had her afternoon off this week and could only spare him a few sneaked minutes but he was more than happy; any time spent with Martha was better than none at all. They had been stepping out for a time and Bob knew without doubt that she was the one for him. Her hair, her smile, her smell – he loved everything about her.

Martha appeared, looking round nervously. Bob stepped out from behind the bushes to get her attention then stepped back. Hoping no one would see and she wouldn't get into trouble, one hand holding her blonde hair that was pulled back and pinned into a bun, she ran lightly across the lawn into his waiting arms. He swept her off her feet, embracing passionately amid the scent of the purple flowers.

Martha felt safe and secure in Bob's strong embrace, hidden by the cover of the rhododendron bushes. She was impatient for his kisses but her mood changed when he put her down and mentioned the war.

In the few minutes they shared, he spoke of nothing else and told her he was seriously thinking of enlisting. She told him not to be a fool, a stupid fool, and made him promise he wouldn't do anything so stupid. Then she had to leave, departing with a little wave of her fingers and running back to the manor. He promised, but later in the pub things were different.

The Swan and Cemetery was crowded when he got there. The next day was a Sunday, a day when the men didn't have to get up early for work. They were making the most of it, determined to enjoy themselves after a hard week. The ale was flowing freely.

Bob looked over the heads for Joe but couldn't see him. He saw two men he recognised, though, over by the bar: Nathanial Bradshaw and Bert Hartley. He knew Mr Hartley from the dairy and Mr Bradshaw through Nathanial's son, Ned. Bob was older than Ned, but that didn't stop the two of them hanging around together from time to time, especially since Joe had got himself married.

Joe Wilson, a joiner by trade, had been down south on a construction job. While he was working there he met up with a London lass called Mary Fennell. They now had a beautiful little daughter, Agnes, and another child on the way. Some said it was a shotgun wedding but Joe seemed more than happy to stay at home with his young family; when he did get out, he never missed an opportunity to proudly open his wallet and show off the photograph inside of Mary and the baby, telling everyone, 'Little Agnes is beautiful, takes after her mother.'

Mr Hartley had his back to the door when Bob came in but Mr Bradshaw saw him and waved him over. 'What you for, young Bob?'

'A pint of bitter, please, Mr Bradshaw.'

'Are you ready for another, Bert?'

Bert downed the last bit of ale in the bottom of his glass in one gulp. 'Aye, go on, Nat. Won't say no.'

While Nathanial ordered the beer, Joe Wilson came in, spotted Bob with Mr Hartley and Mr Bradshaw and made his way over to join them. Nathanial spoke up, 'I'll be right in thinking you'll want a pint of bitter as well, Joe?'

'Thanks, Mr Bradshaw. I could murder a pint,' replied Joe gratefully.

As Nathanial turned back to the barman, Mr Hartley chipped in. 'Eh up, lad, it shouldn't be pints you are talking about murdering, it should be the bloody Germans. Meself and Nathanial are off to sign up tomorrow; t'war's been going on long enough, tha knows. Looks like it needs the likes of me and him to go and sort t'buggers out and put an end to it.'

That was the start of it. The four of them stood round the bar until closing time, drinking and talking about nothing else except Kitchener's latest speech and how it was time they went and served their country.

The recruitment office was inside the town hall. Next morning the Union Jack flew proudly from the flagpole outside the building as Nathanial, Bert, Bob and Joe queued in a long line of men who were waiting to go in.

Bob was the first of them to stand in front of the recruitment officer. He was a bull of a man, with slicked-back hair and a bushy moustache, ends curled to a point. Bob thought the war wouldn't last much longer with men like him fighting 'on our side'.

From behind his desk the sergeant asked, 'Name, date of birth, next of kin.' Having dutifully written down Bob's details, he twiddled his moustache as he looked up and said, 'You're now in the army, young man. Next.'

Bob stepped to one side and another soldier, a clerk, slid a single railway docket across the desk saying, 'There'll be a train leaving for camp tomorrow morning at seven. Make sure you're on it.'

For the next six weeks they were billeted down on the Welsh coast, drilled daily, marched up and down. They performed endless physical fitness exercises and were shown, together with a smattering of basic field skills, how to handle and fire a rifle.

It was down to the railway station after that to be packed on board a train destined for the docks and shipped over to France on an old cattle boat that stank to high heaven. The stench was even worse by the time they landed. Most of the troops were seasick. Bert and Nathanial were two of the worst but Bob enjoyed the crossing. He had never been on a boat before and spent most of the time on deck looking at the white-crested waves and watching the seagulls as they trailed behind, gliding in the ship's wake.

The ship docked in Calais and the troops disembarked. The officers stayed in hotels and guesthouses in and around the town while the men camped in a farmer's meadow, sleeping under canvas. Three days later, they decamped and moved on up to the front.

Bob set off to fight, head held high, chest puffed out. He whistled and sang with the rest of the troops as they marched along the tree-lined avenues, the poplars swaying gently in the light breeze to accompany the rhythm of the soldiers' swinging arms. But sullen silence replaced the men's swagger as they came upon the pitiful hordes staggering towards them. Stretching out as far as the eye could see, lines of men swathed in bloody bandages, injured comrades leaning on injured comrades, wearily putting one foot in front of the other; horse-drawn wagons full of those too maimed to walk, all making their way slowly along the crowded roads heading back to Calais and passage home.

As the recruits passed by the trails of wounded, Martha's words struck home. 'Don't be a fool, don't be a stupid fool,' and

Bob's arms didn't swing so high.

He reached the front and faced the enemy's bullets, their barrage of artillery fire; saw men fall, mown down by machine guns; others hurled into the air by exploding shells, like whirling, stringless marionettes; bodies torn limb from limb by white-hot shrapnel, their bloody stumps raining down about him. With bedlam all around, he sank down, shut his eyes tightly, only to see Martha screaming, 'You promised, you promised!' Guilty, unable to look upon her, he opened his eyes and pressed into the muddy wall of the trench, taking cover and trying not to see.

Between the shelling and the fighting, there were the rats. They were everywhere, rats as big as cats. You could find no peace from them. No sooner had Bob shut his eyes than they would be about him, gnawing at the leather of his boots and uniform. On waking, the first things he saw were razor-sharp teeth, black snouts twitching and beady pink eyes watching him coldly.

Bob didn't like to shut his eyes nor did he like what he saw when he opened them.

Worst of all, though, were the lice. Festering, transparent little things they were, black when bloated with blood and swollen up to the size of a pea. Any time there was a lull in the fighting Bob, Nathanial, Bert and Joe huddled together in the wet, muddy trench and ran a candle down the seams of their uniforms to kill the blighters. No sooner had you got rid of them than they were back.

The four of them stuck solidly together through these insufferable conditions, inseparable, helping and confiding in one another as only those knowing death can come at any second can do. Each nightmare of a day unfolded into the next, each day a struggle to survive, each day wondering if today was going to be their last – but somehow they endured and for nearly two years managed, against all odds, to stay alive.

Then their luck ran out.

A new commanding officer arrived. They knew him; they had often seen him riding about town, in and out of the woods and fields with his brother, the Peculiar Man.

On the same day that he took charge, Joe received a letter from back home. It was from his father-in-law. He had come up from London to pay Mary and the children a visit. While he was there, there was a zeppelin raid; a stray bomb had fallen on the house. Mary was in hospital. The doctors said she would pull through but he was sorry to write that both children, Agnes and Maud, had been killed. They were asleep in their little wooden cots when the bomb fell. Joe got compassionate leave and travelled home for their funerals.

Joe went straight from the train station to the hospital where he found Mary bandaged, pale and drawn, a poor soul, but sitting up in bed. When he put his arms round her, the tears flowed from both of them, an outpouring of grief at the loss of their little girls.

Drying her eyes, Mary told him, 'You've come just in time. They are letting me out today. Dad's coming to collect me soon and has managed to get us a temporary place to live.'

Two days after moving into the grubby little bedsit, they held a service in the local church. Joe always said that being in the trenches was nothing compared to holding Mary's hand that day and seeing his little girls' tiny coffins lowered into the ground. That was hell.

Chapter 41
MUSTARD GAS

FOR DAYS IT hadn't stopped raining. They were wading knee deep through mud, piling sandbags, strengthening trench walls, when orders came to relocate and reinforce the lines near Ypres. The officers went round informing the men to stop work, to go pack their kit.

As Bob, Nathanial and Bert gathered up their few possessions, Joe suddenly turned up. He had been away for only seven days but to his friends it seemed like an eternity. The four men had been inseparable for the past two years; it had felt incomplete without him. But they didn't have time to exchange words; no sooner did Joe appear than the sergeant gave the signal and they set off in the pouring rain. Silently, so as not to give away their position, they waded through the waterlogged and muddy trenches, heads bent low as they travelled along the lines, concealing their movements from the enemy.

They reached Ypres and were held in reserve for four days, giving them plenty of time to catch up, express their sorrow and try their best to raise Joe's spirits. They could not hide their eagerness for any snippet of news from back home however. Joe did his best to tell them all he could but with the funeral and all, he hadn't a great deal to say.

Bob asked if he had seen Martha. 'Only when she attended

the funeral, Bob. She was looking well but I didn't really get a chance to speak to her, just to thank her for coming. She asked after you and I told her you were doing fine and forever talking about her.'

At the end of the four days, they moved on up to Passchendaele.

With the pounding of relentless artillery fire ringing in their ears, they fought furiously for days on end. The field of battle turned into a barren, pockmarked swamp of stagnant, water-filled craters, skeleton trees and human carnage. Then at last a day came when the guns fell silent and a lull in the fighting gave the troops a chance to rest. The men found relief in the quiet stillness, welcoming the cool wind blowing towards them, a change from the searing heat of exploding artillery shells.

Joe, Nathanial, Bert and Bob found some comfort sprawled out over a pile of sandbags. Joe and Bob ran a candle over their uniforms to kill the infestations of lice; Nathanial read a book and Bert stretched out on his back, helmet down over his eyes, asleep.

Suddenly Nathanial stopped reading and glanced up. Bert woke, pushed back his helmet. A faint buzz, a droning noise, grew louder. Instantly all four dived for cover. Shell after shell rained down and erupted, releasing a chemical cocktail of deadly gas. A dense cloud formed, rolling up eerily from the ground, the wind blowing it towards them. Along the trenches, whistles sounded, the signal for the troops to don their masks.

The gas masks were terribly uncomfortable, unbearably hot and sweaty; there was a great temptation to take them off but Nathanial, Bert, Joe and Bob endured. They peered out through the little glass windows that covered their eyes, sucked air through the filtered canister, waited, slowly waited as, with hearts thumping, the deadly mist rolled towards them.

Then a miracle happened: the cloud started to tremble, to flutter and recede as the wind changed direction. The gas blew over no man's land, directly back at the Germans. The men felt a great urge to remove their masks and cheer but they waited for the all-clear to sound; all except for one, their commanding officer, the Peculiar Man's brother. Suddenly he appeared on top of the trench. One hand waving his pistol, with the other he removed his gas mask, threw it to the ground in full view of the troops and next moment screamed, 'CHARGE!' Then he took off, running like a mad March hare towards the enemy.

Nathanial had witnessed the insane carnage and madness of war for the last two years and had kept his counsel but this insanity was too much, even for him. He jumped up and faced the troops from the top of the trench. He also removed his gas mask so that he could be heard. He yelled out for them to stay where they were then glanced round quickly, holding them with his steely glare. Seeing no one move, he turned and sprinted after the Peculiar Man's brother.

The bond between the four men was too great. While all the troops around them remained in the trenches, Joe, Bert and Bob leapt up to help and raced after Nathanial.

The Peculiar Man's brother reached the receding blanket of deadly gas. Nathanial made a desperate lunge and pulled him down on top of him. Joe, quicker than the others, was right there; he kicked the gun out of the Peculiar Man's brother's hand and then kicked him in the head for good measure, knocking him out cold.

Joe did a strange thing then: he took off his gas mask and placed it over the head of the Peculiar Man's brother. Bert and Bob arrived and helped Nathanial up.

'Come on, let's get this bugger back,' Bert said. Together the four of them hauled the unconscious officer back over no man's land under cover of the poisonous cloud and threw him down into the trench.

A senior officer, having observed the whole incident, made his way over. Lifting up the bottom of his gas mask, he nodded down at the Peculiar Man's brother. 'Someone find a stretcher for this clown.' Then he added, 'And you lot, no doubt you'll be getting a mention in dispatches for what you did. Well done, lads. Move sharpish now and get along to the medical station. Have someone look you over.'

The officer continued walking calmly through the packed trenches, holding his gas mask slightly ajar, saying as he went, 'Now, boys, don't you do anything stupid like me and raise your masks until you hear the all-clear.'

The nearest medical station was about half a mile away. By the time they reached it, Joe and Nathanial could hardly see because their eyes were stinging so badly. Bert got a medical officer to attend to them. The doctor did not seem unduly concerned. He instructed an orderly to bathe their eyes in saline water and said, 'Once the orderly has seen to you, find a place to bed down. Try to get some sleep and rest your eyes, then come back and see me in the morning.'

The doctor looked over Bert and Bob. 'Nothing the matter with you, boys. Nevertheless, the same applies to you two: rest up here for the night but make sure you're back with your unit by first light.'

Bert found a place underneath a nearby hedge away from the medical tents where they could all shelter. They made themselves as comfortable as they could and settled down. They slept off and on but by dawn they were all too uncomfortable; yellow blisters covered their bodies. Joe and Nathanial were the worst. Joe could hardly speak because his throat was so swollen and creamy pus filled his and Nathanial's eyes; they could barely see.

Bert went off again to find a medical officer. The doctor took one look at Bert and saw the livid yellow blisters all over his face. 'You're one of the chaps I saw yesterday, aren't you? Come here, let me have a closer look at you.'

'No,' said Bert. 'I'm not too bad. First come and see the others.

They're a lot worse off.'

'Right, let's go.'

Bert led the doctor back over to the hedge. The doctor registered their discomfort but their symptoms were new to him; he had never seen their like. He gave them a cursory examination, asking questions as he looked them over. When he heard they had been involved in a gas attack he raised his eyebrows and, reaching into the pocket of his white coat, brought out a small notebook. As he started to write, he shouted for an orderly.

A man popped his head out from a nearby tent in response to the doctor's call. As he came over, Nathanial doubled up in agony, vomiting.

The doctor did his best for Nathanial but was aware he could do very little for him here. He tore the page from his notebook on which he had written:

MEN INVOLVED IN GAS ATTACK. SYMPTOMS UNKNOWN. POSSIBLY NEW TYPE OF CHEMICAL GAS. IF PROGNOSIS CORRECT ENSURE HQ NOTIFIED.

The doctor handed the note to the orderly and said, 'Get these men on a wagon and down to the hospital. Make sure you give this to the attending officer.'

The hospital was an old, large, rambling chateau given up to the British Army and quickly converted to cater for the sick and wounded. It took a day and a night of driving across the muddy terrain and carefully keeping to the wooden boards put over the worst of the boggy ground for the horse-drawn wagon to get there. By the time they arrived, Bert and Bob were covered in painful pustules but Nathanial and Joe were in a far worse state. Joe could hardly see for the large yellow blisters that covered his eyes and he could not speak, so badly was his throat swollen. Nathanial was even worse. His condition was pitiful; he lay in his own vomit and excrement, permanently doubled up in the back of the wagon, sightless eyes oozing pus.

Outside the hospital, stretcher parties came down and lifted them one at a time and carried them inside. Nurses cut off their uniforms and washed and deloused them before treating their blisters with bleaching powder and white petroleum jelly. Nathanial and Joe also received injections of morphine.

A nurse led Bert and Bob down several long corridors to a wardroom somewhere near the back of the building. Nathanial and Joe were put on trolleys and wheeled off to some other part of the hospital.

Chapter 42
INSIDE THE HOSPITAL

THE HOSPITAL WAS already crowded when they arrived and it filled to overflowing as the gas attacks escalated. The medical staff, exhausted with the number of wounded, were frustrated by how little they could do to help the victims of the attacks. It was heartbreaking for the nurses to see the condition of the soldiers as they arrived, covered in great bleeding blisters, doubled up in pain, always fighting for breath, blind, their eyes stuck together by congealed pus. It wasn't pleasant for Bert and Bob either; seeing the casualties, they realised how lucky they had been but it also made them anxious for Nathanial and Joe. They constantly asked the doctors and nurses about their friends but each time were assured they were in good hands and doing as well as could be expected.

By the third week Bert and Bob were able to get out of bed and move around and they wanted more than just to hear that Nathanial and Joe were doing well; they wanted to see for themselves. Late one night they left their beds and went up to see the duty nurse at her desk at the top of the ward. She had her head down and was writing up notes when they approached. So as not to disturb the other patients, Bert kept his voice just above a whisper. 'Excuse me nurse.'

The nurse looked up at the two men and paused for a moment

before she replied. 'You can call me Mary,' she said. 'But you know you both shouldn't be out of bed at this time of night.'

'I'm sorry, Mary. It's just that Bob and me are fed up being cooped up all day. We wanted to go outside for five minutes and catch a breath of fresh air, if you don't mind,' Bert half lied.

'I'm afraid I'll get into trouble if I agree to that,' Mary replied. But Bert wasn't taking no for an answer and pleaded and cajoled with the young nurse until finally, exasperated, she gave in. 'Okay. The two of you will get me shot. Five minutes and no more, mind you.'

Dressed only in white hospital gowns and army boots, their arms and legs held apart to avoid rubbing the irritating blisters, they went up and down the corridors, peering into room after room, moving like a pair of snooping, overgrown penguins. They soon found Joe; he appeared to be fast asleep. They were delighted to see him but remained at the entrance, peeking in through the window in the door. With all the comings and goings, they did not wish to disturb him; they knew how hard it was to get a good night's sleep in this place.

Now they had found Joe, they continued to search for Nathanial but there was no sign of him. Not wishing to push their luck and get the young nurse into trouble, they waddled back to their ward, believing they might have better luck the following day.

The next night Bert and Bob went to the young nurse again. They said they had seen Joe and asked if they could pay him a short visit. 'Certainly not,' Mary said. 'If the nurse on duty sees you there, I'll be reported for sure.'

Once again they refused to take no for an answer and continued to pester her until she gave in. 'Listen, you two, I'll tell you what I will do. When I go for my break I'll see if I can find the nurse on duty on your friend's ward and I'll have a word with her. If she agrees to let you see him, you can go. But if not, that is the end of the matter. Agreed?'

'Agreed, lass. We can't ask fairer than that now, can we, Bob?' Bert replied with a grin.

The young nurse came back after her break. Bert and Bob waited until her replacement had left before they returned to speak to her.

'You two again,' she said with a smile. 'Before you say anything, yes, I did have a word with the nurse on your friend's ward and yes, she has agreed to let you come and see him. It appears he is to be shipped home tomorrow.'

'Lucky bugger,' Bob and Bert blurted out in unison.

The nurse's smile faded. 'Not that lucky, I'm afraid. It appears that his throat has been badly damaged and it's unlikely that he will ever be able to talk again.'

'You mean he'll be a mute,' exclaimed Bob.

'I'm so sorry,' said the nurse.

'Can we go and see him now?'

'Yes,' she nodded.

'You'll soon be home, Joe, to a roaring fire and a plate of your Mary's cooking,' said Bert jovially as he and Bob stood smiling by the side of Joe's bed.

Joe smiled back and mimed that he had a knife and fork in his hands, pretending to tuck in to a juicy bit of meat. All three knew they weren't fooling anyone. They had been through too much together to do that. They were smiling on the outside but inside Bob and Bert felt like weeping as they watched their friend move his lips without making a sound.

Joe, pleased as he was to see them, hoped they wouldn't stay long. He was in too much pain to keep up this act for much longer; he did not want his friends to see how he was suffering.

While they were there, Bert and Bob asked about Nathanial. Had Joe seen him? Did he know where he was? Joe shook his head but pointed to a bed across the other side of the room. In it was the Peculiar Man's brother.

Joe was starting to mime that the chap wasn't right in the head when the nurse came along and interrupted. 'I think Joe is trying to tell you that the officer over there is slightly troubled. He's going home tomorrow too, but don't think you can spend time talking with him as well. You've already outstayed your welcome.'

'We were just about to leave, nurse. Thanks for letting us visit,' Bert replied.

'Off you go then, shoo, shoo, shoo.'

As Bert and Bob said their goodbyes and the nurse bustled them out of the ward, Joe put his head back down on the pillow and his face screwed up in pain.

Chapter 43
NATHANIAL

WITH JOE ON his way home, Bert and Bob now focused on finding Nathanial. They made it their mission, taking every opportunity to search for him. For a while their efforts drew a blank. Then, more by chance than design, they came upon him.

Snooping around the hospital, they felt certain they had looked everywhere. They were rapidly coming to the conclusion that Nathanial, like Joe, must have been shipped home, when a nurse came towards them in the corridor, struggling with a large wicker basket full of bloodstained sheets. The nurse was behind schedule and knew she would get a telling off from the matron if she arrived late for duty on the ward.

Seeing two men in front of her who appeared fit enough for the task, and hoping to save time, she asked them if they wouldn't mind taking the basket down to the cellar and leaving it outside the boiler room for the caretaker to put into the incinerator.

Eager to help a young, attractive nurse, Bert and Bob said yes. They each took hold of a handle as the nurse thanked them and dashed off, hoping to reach her ward in time.

Bob and Bert went down the steps and carried the laundry basket into the cellar as they looked for the boiler room. There was little light down here and the noise of the boiler and other machinery made conversation difficult. In the semi-darkness, they saw light flickering out from an open door; there were several baskets full of laundry piled up outside. As they walked to the door, they heard screaming coming from up ahead. Puzzled, they dropped the laundry basket and went to see what was going on.

The noise was coming from a small room. They looked inside through the window in the door. Men were lying tied to their beds, leather straps about their wrists and ankles. As they looked around, they saw Nathanial. He started to scream.

Bert barged through the door with Bob at his heels. They ran to Nathanial and started to release the buckles on the straps.

'Nat, it's Bert and Bob,' Bert said. 'We're here now, we'll get you out. We're here now. You'll be alright. We'll see to you.' Nathanial continued screaming.

They heard a nurse's stern voice behind them shouting, 'Stop that at once! You don't know what you are doing.' She pushed her way between Bob and Bert and grabbed at their hands to stop them undoing the buckles.

A doctor joined the fray and pushed Bert and Bob aside. Bert was about to land him a punch but stopped short, furious, as the doctor put his hand up to deflect the blow.

With clenched teeth the doctor said, 'Do that, my man, and you will be in serious trouble.' It was enough to stop Bert but he looked on livid as the doctor added, 'Now what's going on? You two shouldn't be down here.'

'I'll tell you what's going on, mate. We're getting our pal out of here right now. He's in agony and you bastards are doing sod all to help him,' Bert raged.

'Now calm down,' said the doctor, 'and that's an order. There is a lot you don't understand.'

'Try telling us, then,' Bert spat out.

'Calm down and I'll try my best.'

'We're listening.'

'It might not appear so but we are doing our best to treat your friend. These symptoms are new to us. We don't fully understand what's going on. Until we can come up with a form of treatment, the best we can do is try to keep him as still as possible so he cannot inflict more injury upon himself.'

'He's in bloody agony,' raged Bert. 'You can give him something for the pain at least.'

'You don't understand,' said the doctor, his voice softer and tinged with sorrow. 'We only have limited supplies of morphine. What we have must be accounted for and used on the patients that have a chance of pulling through.'

Bert went white as the words sank in. 'You mean Nat is dying and you are letting him die like this?'

'As I've explained, until we can find a cure...' The doctor's voice trailed off.

'There must be something you can do,' Bob pleaded.

The doctor looked down sadly, resigned to the fate of the men in his care and the room went eerily quiet. A moment later he spoke, breaking the silence. 'If your friend here,' he nodded at Bert, 'were to go over to the nurse's desk, pick up the chair behind it and threaten to bash me over the head unless I unlocked the medicine cabinet and administered some morphine, I couldn't be held responsible, could I? I would, however, have to put you both on a charge and fill in the necessary paperwork but that could take some time to process. You two may well be back at the front before it passes through all the channels.'

Bert went over and picked up the chair.

The doctor filled a syringe. Only the nurse noted the extra-large dose and knew for certain his act of kindness. Bob and Bert looked on as the doctor administered the injection. Then Bert sat down on the side of the bed, holding his old friend's hand. They remained with Nathanial as his breathing grew more shallow. Then there was one rasping breath and after it nothing, nothing at all. Nathanial was gone.

As they left Nathanial's side, the doctor said quietly, 'Names please, for the charge sheet.'

'Bert Hartley and Bob Brown,' they answered and thanked the doctor as they went out into the shadowy passageway and headed for the stairs back to their ward.

Chapter 44
The Letter – a Line or Two

ABOVE THE FIREPLACE, the hands of the clock continued to sound the passing of time … tick, tock, tick, tock … and in the growing darkness, Bob Brown sat all alone at the top of the stairs with only his memories.

Eleventh of November 1918, Armistice Day, and somehow he and Bert had survived the war. They were on their way home but they were not the same men who had set out some three years before; after what they had been through, how could they be?

Bert went straight home to his loving wife and the next day pumped up the tyres of his old bicycle and rode over to see Nathanial's wife and son. After that, he rode straight down to the Swan and Cemetery where he found Bob drunk. Bert decided to join him and since that day had never stopped.

A hazy, drunken memory of that afternoon in the Swan and Cemetery was all Bob had left but in his mind he could still hear Bert slurring his words and telling him, 'If you love the girl, marry her. If you don't, you'll regret it but, whatever you do, don't have kids. You'll only be producing cannon fodder for the army.'

That was the trouble though: Bob had returned home to find out the love of his life, Martha, was pregnant with someone else's child.

Bob took Bert's advice and on Martha's next half-day off he went round to see her. She still professed she loved him with all her heart. He had no doubt whatsoever that he loved her, so before Martha's child was born Bob got down on one knee alongside the rhododendron bushes in the grounds of the Peculiar Man's stately manor and proposed. They were married inside a week by the same vicar who performed the funeral service for Joe and Mary's two little girls.

Martha's baby had an enlarged heart when it was born, poor mite. Two months later it died. After that, things between Bob and Martha became difficult. He could see she was deeply troubled and assumed it was to do with the death of the baby. He was willing to give things time until they sorted themselves out but Martha was more troubled than Bob thought.

One morning, shortly after the death of the baby, Martha carried a stepladder to the top of the stairs. Standing under the wooden panel that led up into the loft, she climbed the ladder, pushed open the panel and climbed through. She tied one end of a rope round a roof beam, the other round her neck and dropped back through the opening. A letter fell from her hand.

Bob came home from the dairy as usual in the afternoon. He opened the front door of the terraced house; movement from up the stairs caught his eye. He looked up to see his wife swinging from the end of a rope.

Martha had told Bob she loved him with all her heart; Bob had loved Martha with all his heart. She was the one thing he thought about every day when he was away fighting at the front. She was his salvation; he knew that without her and her letters from home, he would never have survived The Great War. Now she was gone. How would he survive without her?

Bob had seen men torn limb from limb by white-hot shrapnel, cut down by machine-gun fire, their remains devoured by rats. He had seen lice swell and grow fat on his blood, had seen his friend

Nathanial screaming in agony, his friend Joe lying in the street with a bullet hole in his head. Now he saw his beloved Martha hanging with a noose round her neck.

He read her letter and now saw, too, that he had helped save the man who had raped her.

My Dearest Bob,

I love you too much to keep on hurting you. You deserved someone so much better.

Please believe me when I tell you I would have kept myself for you, my dearest, and am truly ashamed that I was not pure on our wedding day. I know you asked me to name the baby's father but believe me, you knowing would have done no good, for what can the likes of us do against them? However, now my duty as a mother to that ill-conceived baby has died along with the child. I have decided my fate and feel it right that I reveal the truth so perhaps you can forgive me and remember me with fondness when I am gone.

I was sent to prepare one of the guest rooms. I didn't know it was for the Peculiar Man's brother. He was injured in the war and coming to the manor to convalesce. When he arrived, he was in a dreadful state, covered in ugly yellow pustules, his mind unclear. As instructed, I brought his meals, made his bed and helped him wash and shave. I never liked going to his room. He was always sullen and never spoke. When I was attending to him, I often spoke of you to settle my nerves and told him how after the war we were going to get married. One day while I was making up his room, I was telling him how you had won a medal and how I was so proud of you. He went crazy and grabbed hold of me. He bashed my head against the wall and started hitting me. I could not fend him off. I tried so hard my dearest, believe me. I scratched and clawed but I could not get away. I thought he was going to kill me and I wish he had instead of doing what he did. Afterwards I had no one to turn to. You were away at war and if word of what had happened got back to the Peculiar Man and his wife, I would have lost my position and been turned out onto the streets.

There was a terrible flu virus going around and lots of people were sick so I took to my room, pretending I was sick too. I lay low until the bruising on my face died down and no one would ask any awkward questions. Later I discovered I was pregnant. You know the rest.

My dearest Bob, I love you truly but can no longer go on living with the shame. Please forgive me.

Your ever loving

Martha

Bob's eyes had been truly opened and he had seen enough. He did not want to see any more.

As the fireplace clock struck nine thirty, Bob folded the letter, placed it back in its envelope and left the house. He didn't bother to close the door, just walked straight out into the darkness. At nine thirty-five, he climbed a fence and slid down a banking overgrown with brambles and weeds. At nine thirty-seven, Bob lay down across the railway tracks behind his rented two-up, two-down house, and waited for the nine-forty express. He didn't have long to wait.

He didn't see the train coming.

Chapter 45
A NEW DAWN

SAM HELPED THE milkman deliver the milk and collect the money on Saturdays. He was the only one in his family who worked and brought money regularly into the house. Sam was eight years old and he worked every day except for Sunday, the Lord's Day, when no one worked as far as Sam knew. Even his dad, who was desperate for a proper job and the money it would bring, who worked wherever and whenever he could, did not work on the Lord's Day.

'You can't put a price on a man's soul, Sammy,' his dad used to say. 'And no man should have the impertinence to try and buy what already belongs to God.'

Sam got out of the bed he shared with his three brothers and elder sister, Sofia. He tried his best to leave the room quietly; he did not want to wake them up. Somehow, though, Sofia always opened her eyes and waved him a gentle goodbye.

Sam crept downstairs to the kitchen. His mum was already there, waiting as she was every morning. Sam pulled out a stool, sat down and, with both hands wrapped round the seat, hitched it forward until his legs were firmly under the small round table and his elbows resting comfortably on top. His mum put down a piece of bread and dripping in front of him and a mug of milk. The milk came from the bottle he had put down his trousers before he left the dairy. He knew it was wrong to steal the milk but all the boys did it; they said it was part of their wages.

Sam hurried as he ate his bread and dripping and drank up his milk; he did not want to be late for work. If he was late he could lose his job; he knew many boys who had. There was not much chance of Sam being late though. Sam was the type of boy who hated to be late for anything.

He put down his empty mug, pushed in his stool and rushed out of the house. His mum stood at the front door and waved him off as he shot along down the street and shouted back, 'Bye, Mum.'

Sam got to the dairy and looked round for Mr Hartley – Bert. Sam and Bert worked together. Sam really liked Bert and Bert really liked Sam. The two of them got on well but not all the time. Sam did not like Bert on Saturdays; Saturday was collection day, the day they went round the customers to get the money for the milk they had delivered through the week. No, Sam did not like Bert on a Saturday.

Wilkinson's paid their employees on a Friday afternoon. Bert collected his money then went straight to the pub. In the pub, he laughed and joked, talked to everyone until his money was spent or he fell down drunk. The landlord and some of the locals would carry him home and put him to bed. The landlord and the locals were good like that. Everyone liked Bert, especially the landlord; Bert was his best customer.

How Bert managed to turn up for work the next day and do his job nobody knew, except Sam. Bert would arrive and then he left everything to Sam while he lay down in the milk cart and slept off his hangover. Sam hated the way Bert talked gibberish when he arrived and smelled of booze and snored loudly and did nothing to help. This was why Sam did not like Bert on Saturdays.

Sam had told his dad about Mr Hartley always being drunk on a Saturday and not doing any work. Sam's dad just said, 'Mr

Hartley is a good man. He fought in The Great War and has been through a lot and he's entitled to have a drink. Be a good boy for Mr Hartley and show him some respect.'

Today wasn't a Saturday. As Sam arrived at the dairy, Mr Hartley saw Sam before Sam saw him and shouted over. Sam ran to him.

'Sam, we're having a bit of a change today.'

'What do you mean, Mr Hartley?' asked Sam.

'Just been told we're getting a new horse.'

'Why are we getting a new horse? I don't want a new horse, Mr Hartley. I like Old Dobbin.'

Sam had spent ages with Old Dobbin after the delivery rounds, rubbing him down, brushing his tail, telling him all his secrets. A few times, after he'd made sure no one was looking, he had even got up on Old Dobbin and pretended he was a cowboy riding in the Wild West and shooting Red Indians. Him and Old Dobbin were pals, he certainly didn't want a new horse, but Sam's dad had told him to be good for Mr Hartley. Sam was going to be good because he was proud that he brought money into his household and he didn't want to lose his job, so he said no more about Old Dobbin.

Bert and Sam walked round the back of the dairy to the stable block. 'I've been told t'horse we got to use is in stall number eight,' said Bert.

Bert unbolted the door to the stall and looked in. Sam had never seen such a pitiful-looking animal. Its black mane and tail were matted, its coat was dusty and its big head hung down wearily. It did not come forward to greet you like Old Dobbin did. Sam took one look at the horse and decided he didn't like it. He said, 'Look at it, Mr Hartley. Look at it. I doubt whether it will even be able to pull t'cart.'

'You could be right, Sam, but sometimes you shouldn't judge a book by its cover, lad. Anyhow, we'll soon see. Come on then, let's get cracking and get it out and harnessed up.'

Sam did not want to touch the horse because it looked that filthy but he reached up and put his fingers round its greasy halter and walked it over to the milk cart. Bert put its harness on, attached the shafts and together he and Sam rode round to the loading bay.

Three men, their shirtsleeves rolled up, hauled crates of milk along the ramp and loaded them into the cart. Once it was full, off Bert and Sam went across the yard, through the blue gates and out on their rounds.

They had not gone far when Bert turned to Sam. 'Do you know what, Sam, this horse might look a sorry sight but I'm telling you, he ain't half strong. See how fast we're going and t'horse isn't even straining.'

Sam had noticed but he did not care; all he could see was a miserable, dirty animal. 'I don't care how fast he can go, Mr Hartley. Old Dobbin was miles better.'

Bert shrugged and carried on driving.

The week passed quickly and it was soon Saturday. On Saturday, Sam did not have to get up so early; it was collection day and they started later. Nevertheless, he still got up early; all the kids in the street where he lived would be up playing football, cowboys and Indians or hide and seek and he liked to join in and play before he went off to work.

He had once asked Bert why they collected money at a different time from when they delivered the milk. Bert told him, 'Well, there's two reasons for that, Sam. First, everyone is paid on a Friday so they'll have money when we call round. Second, if we were to get them out of bed they might be angry and give us an earful for waking them, especially when we ask for money an' all.'

'Oh,' said Sam, 'I wondered why.'

'Well, now you know,' said Bert.

Anyway, today was Saturday and Sam was outside his house

in the cobbled street, playing football with his three brothers and two other boys. He was not worried about being late for work. He knew his mum would come out and call him in plenty of time.

They had picked sides, three boys on each, and had taken off their jumpers and thrown them down on the cobbles to make goalposts. They were having great fun pretending they were playing in a cup final. Sam had the ball and was about to shoot at the goal when he was tackled. He fell awkwardly, banging his left knee. Just then, his mum came to the door and shouted for him to get a move on, it was time he was off down to the dairy. Sam picked himself up, limped over, got his jumper, put it on and set off for work.

By the time he reached the dairy, his knee had swollen up and was beginning to hurt really badly. He hobbled to the stables and saw that the door to stall number eight was open. He thought at first Bert might have got the mangy horse out and gone without him but then he heard snoring coming from inside. He limped over to the stall and found Bert fast asleep by the side of the horse.

Sam knew he would have to take the horse outside and harness him to the wagon. Looking at the state Bert was in, if he did not do it no one else would, and if they didn't do the collection they could lose their jobs. Sam was too proud to lose his job.

He hobbled into the stall, reached up and caught hold of Bracken's halter. Sam's face screwed up in disgust as he touched the oily, rotting leather. He started to lead Bracken outside but as he did, the horse raised its big head and lifted Sam up off his feet. Sam was too startled to let go of the halter as the horse walked right out of the stall and over to the milk cart and stopped. Sam knew something special had happened, he just didn't know what.

Sam wore a puzzled look on his face as he harnessed the horse to the cart then drove it up as near as he could to the stable block. He managed to get down and limp into the stall, then bent down and shook Bert saying, 'Mr Hartley, Mr Hartley, wake up! It's Sam.

Come on, we've got to do us collection else we'll be in trouble. Come on, Mr Hartley, wake up! We've got to be on us way.'

It was enough to rouse Bert. He opened his bleary eyes, staggered up onto his feet, stumbled out of the door and fell into the milk cart. Sam followed, hopping, and got in.

As Sam drove the milk cart, he hardly noticed the threadbare children in the cobbled streets playing hopscotch, football, skipping and spinning tops. He was busy wondering about the horse. Something strange had happened back at the dairy.

Bert was out cold on the floor of the wagon, reeking of booze and snoring like an old goat. Sam held the reins, though hold them was all he needed to do; Bracken seemed to know exactly where to go and did not need any direction from him. Sam let Bracken pull them to the first house where they started the collection.

Sam gingerly got out of the cart, holding the tally book in his hand. He hopped to the door, knocked and, while waiting for the householder to come, he opened up the tally book to see how much milk they had delivered throughout the week and work out what was due. He knew a pint of milk cost tuppence and he read in the tally book that this house had had four pints delivered, so he worked out that eight pence was owed.

A woman came to the door; she wore a hairnet and a cigarette dangled out of the side of her mouth. She held a small leather purse.

'Milk money please,' said Sam.

'How much is it this week, love?' asked the woman, opening her purse and already counting out the pennies.

'Eight pence, missus.' Sam held out his hand as the woman counted the coins and placed them in his palm.

'Ta, missus,' he said. By the time he had checked the coins, counting them himself to make sure she had given him the right money, and put them into his trouser pocket, the woman had gone back inside and shut the door.

Sam hopped to the door of the next house and knocked. He could hear a man's voice inside. 'That'll be the milk. He'll be wanting money.' Then a woman said, 'I'll go,' and opened the door.

'That will be six pence, please, missus,' Sam said. As she was looking in her purse a little toddler, naked except for a once-white towelling nappy, came and stood between her legs. The child was obviously a little girl; she had beautiful curly blonde hair.

Sam said, 'Hello there, how are you?' The little girl put her thumb in her mouth, sucked it for a moment and then ran back inside the house.

'She's shy, is that one,' said the woman. She gave Sam the money and closed the door.

Sam had a bit further to go to the next house so he held on and leant on the window ledges of the houses, hopping on his good leg. His knee was now very sore and swollen. He knocked at the door and a man came out wearing nothing but a string vest and long white underpants. 'Milk money, please,' said Sam.

'Hang on a minute, son,' the man said and he turned his head and shouted back down the hallway, 'Dora, it's t'milk. He's come for his money. She'll be with you in a tick, son.' The man disappeared inside the house and a woman filled the space he'd left. She wore a patterned pinny over a pink-and-white polka-dot skirt and a knitted pink cardigan. Her brown hair was tied back in a bun.

'How much, love?'

'One shilling and tuppence, please,' answered Sam.

'One shilling and tuppence,' repeated the woman. 'We'll have to start cutting back. We can't afford that. Has t'dairy put price up?'

Before Sam had a chance to answer, she paid him the money and closed the door.

Sam knocked on the next house and then moved on to the

next, again using the window ledges to lean on as he limped round the houses, going from door to door, until he got to the end of the street. By this time it was all he could do to stop himself crying. He was in a lot of pain, could not bend his knee and his head was throbbing something awful. He wanted to go home. He also wanted to punch Bert for being drunk, useless and asleep instead of helping him.

He hopped over to the cart. Bert was still slumped on the floor, snoring. Sam wanted to kick him. He sat down on the bench; at least sitting down, his leg felt a little easier but he still had the other side of the street to do and all the other streets after that.

A tear appeared in Sam's eye but he was not going to cry. He was proud; he was the only one in his house that had a regular job and he was not going to risk losing it. Somehow he would cope. He picked up the reins and, holding back the tears, said almost in a whisper, 'Gee up,' as he turned the horse and cart back round at the end of the street.

Bracken pulled the milk cart round and Sam called out, 'Whoa,' at the same time as he pulled back on the reins. Bracken stopped by the curb outside the door of the first house on the opposite side of the street. Sam was just about to get up off his seat when the milk cart moved forward again. Sam saw Bracken take a step up the curb and cross the pavement to the door. Then he saw Bracken lift his leg and knock three times on the door before stepping back onto the cobbled street again.

Sam was staring dumbfounded at Bracken when a man came out of the house. He said, ''Ere's eight pence lad. I know how much t'milk bill is, same every week.' He put the money into Sam's hand then went back inside. As Sam sat with the coins in his hand, Bracken moved forward and knocked on the next door.

Sam simply could not believe what he was seeing.

''Ow much, love?' said a little grey-haired woman, opening the door.

'Oh,' said Sam from up on the cart, looking down at the tally book. 'You're number thirty-nine, aren't you?' he went on, bewildered.

'Yes, love. Been thirty-nine as long as I can remember, unless t'top screw has come loose and nine turned upside down. In that case I'm number thirty-six.' She laughed at her own joke.

Sam was too taken aback by Bracken to notice her little joke, let alone laugh at it. He just said, 'Four pence, please.'

The grey-haired woman gave him two pennies and one tuppence piece and said, 'Trouble with you young 'uns today is you've no sense of humour,' and slammed the door.

All down the street Bracken knocked on the doors. All Sam had to do was sit in the cart, rest his sore leg and hold out his hand for the money. Down every street they went Sam continued to collect the milk money while Bracken knocked on the doors.

Towards the end of the round, Bert's hangover started to wear off and he woke. His eyelids flickered open and he looked up from the bottom of the footwell where he was sprawled. A confused expression came over his heavily wrinkled face. Sam was sitting there holding out his hand and one customer after another simply put money into his palm.

Something registered in Bert's brain; this was not how things were done. The lad should be down off the wagon, knocking on doors.

Bert pulled himself up and tapped Sam on the shoulder. 'Eh, Sam lad, what you playing at? Who you got knocking on people's doors?'

Sam pointed at the horse. 'He's the knocker.'

Bert turned to look as Bracken went up onto the pavement and rapped lightly with his hoof on the front door of the next terraced house.

'Well I'll be dammed,' said Bert. 'He's THE KNOCKER, all right!'

Chapter 46
ANOTHER PHONE CALL

HIS STORY FINISHED, he stopped talking and looked slowly round the room, seeming to wait for some silent pain to pass. This was the first time I had seen my father in discomfort since he started telling his tale. Hoping to distract him, I asked my question: 'How did you get to know about the Peculiar Man and everything else, Dad?'

'Oh,' he said. 'I forgot that you never knew any of my family, did you?'

'That's right, unfortunately I never did,' I replied. My grandfather and granny died before I was born and my father's two brothers and two sisters emigrated to Australia. I had only ever seen one brother, Wilfred. He came over on vacation and stayed a night or two with us in my dad's house when I was very young. I could barely remember him.

From under the quilt, my father's hand slowly snaked out. It held a paper tissue. He poked it towards the yoghurt carton by the side of the bed. His lips were very dry. I pulled back the silver foil from the carton, stuck in a straw and held it for him. I could see his Adam's apple move up and down and hear him slowly gulp as the yoghurt trickled down his throat. When he finished drinking, the straw slipped from his mouth. I removed the carton and he brought the tissue shakily to his lips and patted them before continuing to tell me how he knew the story.

'Your grandfather was an officer in the First World War and after that he was the Peculiar Man's estate manager. Your Grandma Mary served as a nurse and knew Ned's wife, you see. As for my brothers and sisters, my eldest sister, your Aunty Lillian, was a scullery maid at the manor and your Uncle Wilfred worked as a waiter in a posh gentleman's club in town. I know they didn't have the best jobs in the world but times were hard in those days and you took anything you got. But my youngest sister, Margery, she had a good job. She worked in Wilkinson's Dairy as a secretary.'

Somewhat puzzled, I said, 'But I thought you had another brother, Frank, Dad. Did he not have anything to do with the story?'

'Oh, my oldest brother.' He paused before continuing, then said quietly, 'He liked wearing red felt hats.'

Now I knew; the family must have sat around at some time or other and pieced together the whole story between them. I had one last question I simply had to ask. 'What about you, Dad? Did you have any part to play in all this?'

A small grin appeared on his frail face, as if he were remembering. 'Well, I used to play football in the street with Sam before he went off to work.'

I like to think that telling the story did my father some good but it had taken a lot out of him. Or perhaps it was the memory of running round kicking a football with Sam that made him look so tired now; I didn't know for sure and I didn't ask. I knew, however, that he needed to rest. I tucked the duvet under his chin and, as I made him comfortable, he gave a gentle smile, the very effort of which seemed to tire him further. Then he shut his eyes and seconds later he was fast asleep. I made sure the electric blanket was set at the right temperature, left and drove back to my father's house in the red Hyundai.

Back at the house, I put the kettle on to make a cup of tea. It was strange seeing only one cup on the work surface by the sugar bowl; it looked rather lonely. Where was my father's cup I thought as I carried my drink upstairs to bed.

You fear the worst when the phone goes late at night.

I was asleep when the phone rang. Drowsy, in a haze, I reached over, fumbled as I put it to my ear and heard a voice. A voice I recognised from the care home, the voice of a female telling me, 'Your father has passed away.'

⚸ ⚸ ⚸

Looking at my father's coffin resting in front of the marble altar, I remembered the night the doctor phoned. She said he had two days to live but he lived longer, long enough to tell a story, a story more about a noble horse than a peculiar man.

Sitting in the quiet of the church, I thought about the tale and imagined Bracken, Dad standing at his side, while the horse knocked gently on heaven's white pearly gates. In the holy silence I then realised there would be no need of Bracken's hooves. Anticipating my father, the Kingdom of Heaven's entrance had been open for a while as the host waited upon him. When he arrived at last, he would be greeted warmly, welcomed inside as the angels impatiently closed the gates behind him.

I walked out of the church into the sunlight. A little robin landed at my feet. It cocked its head and for a moment looked at me.

Then it flew away.

We Knew Him

I knew a man once
A great man
All the world didn't know him
But you and I did

I knew a man once
A great man
A gentleman, a kind
Honest, noble man
Who could walk with his head held high
All the world didn't walk beside him
But you and I did

I knew a man once
A great man
He had a strong handshake
A firm grip
But a gentle touch
All the world never shook his hand
But you and I did

I knew a man once
A great man
He had a kind word for everyone
Gave sound advice
And offered words of comfort
All the world didn't hear him
But you and I did

I knew a man once
A great man
He'd sit a child upon his knee
Children loved him and he loved children
All the world's children
Didn't know his love
But you and I did

I knew a man once
A great man
He delighted in the joys of nature
Daily fed, whistled
And flew with the birds
All the world didn't see him soar
But you and I did

I knew a man once
A great man
A loving husband
A caring father, grandfather
A dear, dear friend
I knew a man once, a great, great man
That man was our dad

NR 26/06/2013

Postscript
THE DEPRESSION

THE FINANCIAL DISASTER known as the Great Depression started in America towards the end of the 1920s. The share market plummeted, the financial district of New York, Wall Street, crashed and there was an unprecedented run on the banks. America was in economic turmoil and the impact spread across the world.

By early 1930, the financial shock waves reached the shores of the British Isles. Britain's economy was already fragile, trying to recover from the debt and cost of The Great War. It was a country too where the memory of war and the appalling loss of British troops having sacrificed their lives for king and country still lingered, particularly among the working classes, a large proportion of whom were ex-servicemen.

The politicians had promised them a land fit for heroes when the war was over but those who managed to return home found it far from that. They came back to a country with little work and far too few jobs to go round. Then, as Britain's economy struggled to make headway, the Depression hit. Neither the country nor its citizens were prepared for, nor did they deserve, the suffering it wrought.

The jolt was felt immediately, arguably nowhere more so than in the north of England. The demand for coal slumped. Thousands of hard men, coal-faced miners, used to toiling in the shadows of dim lamplight, muscles straining with every swing of the pickaxe and shovel load of coal, found themselves out of work. Yorkshire, with its skyline of colliery winding towers and warren of underground pits, was devastated.

As orders for new tonnage failed to come in, shipbuilding – the only industrial employer of substance on Tyneside – ceased. The men engaged in the shipyards, the draughtsmen working in the drawing offices, the platers, the riveters, the fitters and labourers, were all surplus to requirements. Their employment terminated and, without money coming in, the folk of Tyneside were brought to their knees and suffered terrible hardship.

The people of Lancashire, enduring life amid the polluting cotton mills and dye works, fared no better. Orders for textiles dried up and Manchester, the centre of the textile industry, known as 'Cottonopolis' throughout the world for the volume and the finery it produced, was Cottonopolis no more. Thousands of textile and mill workers across the county were made jobless and, having no income to pay for rent or food, found themselves homeless and starving.

People born and bred in these areas, people whose kith and kin had given their lives in The Great War, whose ancestors had helped forge the industrial revolution and make Britain 'Great', suffered in the Depression like no others. No one was buying the goods they produced and companies, unable to make a profit, closed down. Men, no matter what trade they followed above or below ground, were out of work and millions of the unemployed and their families were left destitute.

Queuing outside charity shops and soup kitchens became a way of life in the 1930s. Once-proud folk had no recourse but to live off scraps and beg for handouts as they watched helplessly as their malnourished children succumbed to the rigours of rickets, scurvy, tuberculosis and death.

Note: All historical facts and details contained within the novel are accurate to the best of my knowledge. However, with reference to the zeppelin raid and killing of the two little Wilson girls, the raid actually took place on Tuesday, 26 September 1916, but in order to fit the time line of the story, I altered the date. During the raid, twelve bombs were dropped but no fatalities were reported.

The author was born in Lancashire, England. Having traveled extensively he now resides in Australia where he describes himself as a 'ping pong pomme', his love of family, friends, football and English beer compelling him to return often to his homeland and place of birth.

You can learn more about the author by visiting his web page http://rigbyjack.wix.com/theknocker